BUT JESUS NEVER WEPT

JUSTINIA WRIGHT PRIVATE INVESTIGATOR
MYSTERIES
BOOK 3

C W HAWES

CWH BOOKS KATY, TEXAS

Cover art by Raihana Dewji

❀ Created with Vellum

This one's for Susannah, Jodi, and Zach.
Thanks for everything.

JOIN THE TEAM!

I invite you to become a VIP Reader. You'll get a free copy of *Vampire House and other early cases of Justinia Wright, P.I.* right off the bat.

Then once a month, maybe more often, you'll get a variety of good things to keep you up to date with my many worlds, as well as curated content.

Just click, tap, or scan the QR code to begin the adventure!

1

SEPPUKU

Tuesday Night, 4 February

A KNIFE IS AN AMAZING INSTRUMENT. IN THE HANDS OF A DOCTOR, IT can lead to healing and health. In the hands of a butcher, it distinguishes cuts of meat. In the hands of a chef, it prepares a tasty meal. And in the hands of a killer, it brings about death.

The scene before us was gruesome. The Reverend Gary Barlow had been tied down spread-eagle on his bed and someone had performed seppuku on him in the shape of a cross. Rather grisly humor that. The reason we knew the victim's name is because nine hours earlier he had been sitting in Tina's office asking her to conduct surveillance on his wife. The reason we were in his bedroom looking at his naked and eviscerated body was because he'd phoned and told us he had something we needed to see. What it was, he hadn't told us. Of course. Isn't that how it always is?

I took out my cell and told it to call "Cal", who is Lieutenant Cal Swenson of Minneapolis Homicide. He answered on the second ring.

"Swenson."

"Hey, Cal. Harry Wright here."

"Hey, Major. What's up?"

"Tina and I are looking at a dead body. He was our client as of a half hour ago." I looked at my watch. "Make that forty minutes."

"Where are you?"

I gave him the address.

"I'll be right there." He ended the call.

Tina and I looked at each other.

She shook her head and said, "Goddamn it. This sucks."

———

That morning had begun like most mornings. I'd made a continental breakfast and let Buddy, Bea's and my little affenpinscher, out so he could do his thing in the yard. In that sense, Tina has it easy. Her three cats simply visit their litter boxes and then Bea or I clean the boxes out once a week. I shouldn't complain because when I moved in with my sister a half-dozen or so years ago, I knew I was signing up to be her Majordomo and head and only servant.

When my beautiful wife of all of six weeks, who is now my partner in servitude, came downstairs, she and I ate pastries, drank tea, and read the paper.

A grumpy Tina had followed Bea by a few minutes and sat at the head of the table. Even though I am the older sibling, my sister is head of the house and always sits at the head of the table. And no one else does. Once seated, she mumbled something, probably a greeting, and promptly stuck her nose in her iPad.

In the three weeks following the conclusion of the Catchfire-Anderson case, Tina and Cal had a spat and he'd moved out. They were still seeing each other, but agreed maybe a bit more distance was best for the relationship.

Bea was crushed. She is so very fond of Cal. Tina didn't show much emotion, but I think she took his move back to his own house rather hard.

She's been very quiet. Spends almost all of her time painting and playing the piano and has turned down no less than fourteen attempts to hire her. One of those attempts was from the Minneapolis Police Homicide Department to consult on a case.

This morning, however, after we'd finished breakfast, Tina announced she'd be in the office. Bea and I looked at each other but said nothing. When I got to my desk, Tina was at hers smoking a cigar and sipping a glass of madeira while reading a book on using drones for surveillance. Since we have two, she wanted to get more use out of them than what we'd gotten to date.

Shortly after ten, Bea poked her head in and said we had a visitor.

Tina looked up, closed the book on a finger, and looked at her cigar. She had half of the thing left. Since she never relights one, I knew the struggle going on in her mind. The struggle between seeing the potential client and finishing the Muniemaker Long. In the end, she let out a sigh and told Bea to show the person in.

Bea left and returned with a tall, broad-shouldered man, who had somewhat of a stocky build. He was dressed in an impeccable charcoal gray suit. She introduced him as the Reverend Gary Barlow.

I stood and said, "I'm Harry Wright and this is my sister, Miss Justinia Wright." I indicated he should have a seat in the oxblood wingback.

His melodious baritone told us he was pleased to make our acquaintance.

Tina spoke. "And what brings you here this morning, Reverend Barlow? The weather is more conducive to sitting by the fire with a good book."

"That it is, Miss Wright, that it is." He cleared his throat. "I would like you to conduct surveillance on my wife."

"Why?" Tina asked.

"I'm not exactly sure."

"An interesting answer. Not sure I've heard that one before."

"I'd think not."

"My rates are very high, Reverend Barlow."

"Yes, I know. I can pay them."

Tina raised her eyebrows.

He went on. "I've checked and everyone says you are the best."

"If you aren't exactly sure why you want me to spy on your wife, in what way are you inexactly sure?"

He smiled. "I like that. Let me see." He looked at the ceiling, or maybe he was trying to see if he could get a direct connect with someone in heaven. Finally he said, "Seven months ago, July, I noticed my wife's behavior was changing. Not a complete change in habits or routines, but enough so I started noticing. She's slowly becoming a different person."

"Is the change for better or for worse?" Tina kept a straight face.

"I can't say either. She's just different. Good pun, by the way."

"Thank you. Do you like how she is?"

He shrugged. "Again, I can't say I like the new Celeste any more or less than the old Celeste."

Tina pursed her lips, looked at her flawless copy of Paul Strand's *Wall Street* hanging on the wall over the fireplace, I suppose hoping the austere gray and black tones might provide her with inspiration, and then looked back at Barlow. She unpursed her lips. "If you are okay with Celeste as she has become, why do you want me to investigate her?"

"I guess I'm curious to know the source or reason for the change."

"You know the saying, let sleeping dogs lie?"

He nodded.

They looked at each other for a good quarter minute.

"Your curiosity will cost you less if you go elsewhere."

"You are, by all accounts, the best."

She sighed and I knew what was coming next. The ridiculous retainer.

"Reverend Barlow, I will need a twenty thousand dollar retainer and I will be charging Celeste's surveillance at one thousand dollars an hour. The hourly rate includes expenses and a partial hour will be charged at the full hour rate."

Barlow had a big grin on his face. "Just like they said. Why don't you want the case?"

That was a new one. The potential client doing sufficient research to know Tina's fee setting habits.

Tina, too, was smiling. "Chalk it up to my proclivity for play rather than work."

"An odd way to run a business."

"Perhaps. Yet I have more business than I need, Reverend Barlow, because, as you observed, I am the best."

"All right. I suppose there is no negotiating?"

Tina shook her head.

"How shall I pay you?"

"Cash, which is preferred, check, or credit card. Harry, give the Reverend a contract."

I gave Barlow a contract and he took out a checkbook and a fountain pen. He read the contract and signed it. I took out the Eversharp Skyline Bea had given me. The one which had belonged to her late hife (a Tina-ism for the partner in a same sex marriage), Alicia Harris, and signed the contract as well.

"A fellow fountain pen user," Barlow observed.

"You bet."

"What ink are you using?"

"Noodler's Bulletproof Black."

"That's what I use."

"Good ink."

"It is indeed. Your pen is unusual."

"Vintage," I said. "Nineteen Forties. Eversharp Skyline."

"Very nice. Mine is a Sailor."

"I have one. 1911M. Very nice pen."

"That it is."

Barlow wrote out the check, waved it in the air so the ink

would dry, and gave it to me, along with an envelope. To Tina, he said, "In the envelope are photos of Celeste and the vital statistics you requested on your website."

"Thank you, Reverend Barlow. Is your wife employed?"

"No. Not outside the home. She resigned her position at the church about five years ago."

"Why?"

"She wanted to pursue other interests."

"What manner of interests?"

"Anything, really. Just nothing religious."

"Crisis of faith?"

"Yes. I guess that's what you'd call it. You see, we came to the conclusion there was no historical Jesus. He's a myth. No different than Mithras, Osiris, or Paul Bunyan."

Tina leaned forward in her chair. "What do you mean? Are you saying Jesus never lived?"

Barlow shifted in his chair. Took on a bit of a professorial air. "The evidence is quite clear, if you step outside of the Christian theological box to examine it. Jesus is at best a compilation of several historical Messianic figures. This amalgam took on a mythic life of its own and became the Jesus of the early Christians and the gospel writers."

Tina leaned back in her chair, her face screwed up in thought.

Barlow went on. "Celeste gave up her faith and religion. She couldn't see believing in what she called a 'fairytale'. I, on the other hand, kept my faith and stayed with the church."

"How are you able to do so if there is no basis for the church and faith?" I asked.

He shrugged. "Simple, really. I took a page out of Bultmann's book, so to speak. It doesn't matter if Jesus was real or not. The core message of faith and salvation, offered in the New Testament, is what is important."

I pondered for a moment what Barlow had said. In a way, it made sense. "So for you, belief is in the message and not in the messenger."

"That's one way to put it. Celeste is not into existentialism. She's very much a materialist. If Jesus wasn't real, then the whole edifice is merely a façade and one she could not, therefore, accept. She wants the house, not a Hollywood fake."

"What did she do to replace her job as a minister?" Tina asked.

"Mostly volunteer work. She also began blogging about her journey out of faith."

Tina shifted in her chair and cast a glance towards the humidor on her desk. "Do you have any children, Reverend Barlow?"

"Yes. A son and a daughter. Robert is a senior and Emily is a sophomore. Both are at Groton-Peabody Academy in Massachusetts."

Aha! These people have money. Couldn't have gotten it from the ministry. At least any ministry I know of.

"So the children aren't here?" Tina asked.

"Correct. Celeste loves her children, but she was never interested in being a full-time mother."

"You're not interested in being a full-time father?"

"I am, Miss Wright. Groton-Peabody is a family tradition."

Yep. Money. Old money.

"Which allows you to not be a full-time father."

Barlow smiled. "Touché! What I meant was, I love my children — as does Celeste — however, I take more of an interest in them personally than she does. Celeste tends to be a bit distant with Rob and Em."

Tina pursed her lips, tilted her head, and cast a glance upwards. She was chewing on that piece of information. Why? I haven't the slightest idea. In a moment she continued on a different line of inquiry. "Does your wife spend much time at home?"

"She maintains odd hours. Nothing definite or predictable. I'd guess maybe half her time she spends at home. But it could be less. When I'm at the office she doesn't check in with me if she goes out."

"So you don't know what she does or where she goes during the daytime."

"Correct."

"And these odd hours began when?"

"About the same time I noticed those small changes in her behavior."

"Do those changes involve new perfume and lipstick colors?"

Now it was Barlow's turn to purse his lips. He glanced at the ceiling. Perhaps invoking divine guidance? When done communing, he said, "I think so, yes."

"Do you have separate bedrooms?"

"Yes. Makes things easier. With her odd hours, she used to wake me at times. Now I can get a full night's sleep."

"You don't worry about her?"

"Well, yes, I do. I suppose that is one reason why I'm here. I want to know what is going on."

"You haven't asked her?"

"Of course, I have. She won't say anything, though. Just assures me she is busy with her causes and is happy."

"Have you considered that your wife might be having an affair?"

"Yes, I've considered it. It was one of the things I asked her and she maintains she is not having an affair. I believe her because I do think she loves me. She has not displayed any behavior that indicates she doesn't."

Tina placed her hands together as in prayer and rested her nose and lips against them in thought. After a few moments she spoke. "I think we're fine for now. Do you happen to know where your wife is?"

"At home. I stopped there before I came here."

"Very good. We'll start right away, Reverend Barlow."

He stood. "Thank you. A good day to you, Miss Wright. Mr. Wright."

We replied in kind.

After the Reverend left, I drove to the Barlow residence in the posh Cedar-Isles neighborhood, taking the envelope of information with me.

I parked several houses down and watched the driveway and front of the house, while looking over the material the Reverend had provided us.

At three, Celeste Barlow left the house in her BMW and drove into downtown Minneapolis. I followed her to The Hotel Minneapolis. She parked in front, the valet took her car, and she went inside. Being winter, I had a look at her coat, some ankle-length thing, and nothing else.

I found a parking spot, plugged the meter, and walked back to the hotel. Once inside, I walked up to the desk and told the clerk I was to meet a friend, Celeste Barlow. The young woman checked the computer.

"I'm very sorry, sir, but we have no one registered under that name."

Whatever Celeste was doing, she wasn't using her real name. Usually that spells *affair*. I took from my coat pocket one of the photos Barlow had given us.

"This woman," I said, showing her the picture.

She shook her head. "I'm very sorry. I don't recognize her."

"Maybe she checked in with one of the others?"

The young woman took the photo and showed it to the two other clerks on duty. When she returned, she said, "I'm sorry, sir."

I thanked her, retrieved the picture and pocketed it, looked around and headed for a comfy looking chair. Once in the chair, I ran over the information Barlow had told us and added to it what I had gotten from the clerk.

Celeste was here, but using a false name. All of the data added up in my head to an affair. The former Reverend Celeste Barlow was cheating on her husband. At least that is how I saw it.

My options were simple: I could wait in the lobby and catch her when she appeared, I could call in reinforcements, or I could call Tina for instructions. I decided to let the boss earn some money and called in for instructions. Since I wasn't in a hurry, I called the office number.

"Wright Investigations."

"Hey, Babe."

"Harry, my love, how sweet of you to call."

"Actually, Honey Bunch, I need to talk to Tina, but wanted to hear your voice."

"You are so sweet. I'll ring you through. Love you!"

"Love you, too."

In a moment I heard, "What do you need, Harry?"

I explained the situation to her and asked for direction.

"Come home. We're going to need more people on this."

"I'm on my way."

I left The Hotel Minneapolis, walked to my car, and drove home.

A little after five, I was walking in the door. Greeting my ears was "Yon rising Moon…", the fifth of Arthur Foote's *Five Poems After Omar Khayyam*. Greeting my nose was the smell of a Swiss Onion Tart. Bea had apparently taken a walk through my recipe file.

Onions, mushrooms, and garlic are probably my three all time favs and the tart is my favorite onion dish. Right behind it are onions baked with rosemary and cream and Pissaladières, which are onion and anchovy tarts.

The latter are actually hors d'oeuvres and I like them a lot, although few others do. Norm was one of those few. But Tina hasn't seen him for quite awhile now. Bea's brother also likes them. He and the family spend most of their time in Provence or Narbona, as it's called in the local Occitan. Most know the city by its French name of Narbonne.

Following my nose to the kitchen, I took a look around. Bea had made, in addition to the tart, a salad and a pot of cream of barley soup, which was simmering on the stove. There was an apple pie resting on the cooling rack. What a busy little beaver my wife's been while I was out.

She wasn't in the kitchen. I went looking for her and found her still at her desk in the office going through paperwork.

"Hey, Babe, you going to work all night?"

"Just finishing up some stuff."

I kissed her and said I'd be in the library. On the way, I stopped in the kitchen, poured myself a glass of Gewürztraminer, and took it with me to the library. I read *Any Human Heart* until supper.

The soup and tart were excellent. Dinner conversation centered around the lousy state the world was in and the general ineptitude of the world's leaders, including our own, in handling the proliferating crises.

However, we didn't get to finish our meal or the discussion because Barlow telephoned, said he had something to show us, and could we come right away. That was twenty minutes before seven and by the time we got out of the house and drove to his place forty minutes had passed. When Tina pulled up to the curb, the first thing we noticed was the front door was open.

"That's odd," Tina remarked and I concurred. After all, we were in Minnesota, in the winter, and a godawful winter on top of it.

We got out of her Crossfire and walked up the walk. It had been shoveled so no footprints showed. We entered, calling Barlow's name. My hand was on my Smith and Wesson Bodyguard revolver. Our search didn't take long.

Whoever killed the Reverend had severed sufficient arteries to enable Barlow to bleed out quickly. Seppuku, if done poorly, can leave a person in agony for quite a long time. The Reverend's killer was at least merciful. He or she was also considerate of the neighbors, for Barlow had been gagged.

While waiting for Cal to arrive, I photographed every room in the house. Just in case we needed pics of the crime scene. Not that I didn't trust the police to take good pictures. I do. I just don't trust them to share.

Our man in blue didn't take long to arrive. When he did he

greeted us. Tina responded with, "Hello, Cal." I simply said "Hey" and stuck out my hand. He took it and we shook hands. I like Cal, consider him a friend, and just because he and Tina are having a lover's quarrel doesn't mean I have to get involved.

Greetings over, he got down to business. "What do you know?"

We gave him the information I've given you. And because those nearest and dearest to us are also those most likely to stick a knife in us, Tina gave him the info we had on Celeste.

He scratched the top of his head. "So the Reverend's wife was at The Hotel Minneapolis, and for now we're saying she still is, under an assumed name."

"Yep," I replied.

He shook his head. "People are damn odd." He sighed. "I suppose I'll have to leave someone here until she returns and probably someone at the hotel."

Not waiting for an answer from Tina or I, he started yelling "Nordquist!" and set off to find said person.

Tina and I waited around for another couple hours but no Celeste and the police were still busy photographing, dusting for prints, and what not.

"Harry, let's go home. We've given our statements and Cal knows where we live."

"Sure. You want me to tell him?"

She nodded.

I got out of my chair and wandered around until I found him. "Hey, Cal, Tina and I are going home."

He had a perturbed look on his face. "She sent you?"

I nodded.

He shook his head and muttered, "Just because of a goddamn cup of coffee." Then he said, "Go ahead, Major. I know where to find you if I need you."

"That you do." I spied Cal's partner, Sergeant Nikki Nelson. She flashed me a smile. She always gives me the impression she'd love to get Cal in the sack and so any tiff between him and Tina seems to put a big smile on her face. I smiled back to keep things friendly. To Cal, I said, "For what it's worth, I think Tina's sorry."

"Then she should say something, don't you think?"

"I do, yes. I'm just giving you info."

"Thanks, Harry, didn't meant to bite your head off."

"There's no offense where none is taken."

He nodded and went back to work.

I found Tina and told her we were good to go. We got into her Crossfire and took off for home. On the way, the only thing she said was, "Why seppuku?"

2

TURNING THE SIMPLE TO COMPLEX

Wednesday, 5 February

I WAS UP EARLY, PRIMARILY TO STOP BY THE BAKERY TO PICK UP pastries for breakfast. On a whim I drove by the Barlow residence after procuring a couple dozen non-healthy delights. The time was a little after six-thirty. I found Officer Nordquist sitting in a squad. I pulled up next to the car and asked if Mrs. Barlow had come home.

"If she had, I wouldn't be here."

He had a point. The temp was a balmy three above zero and the windchill was at eight below. To thank him for the information and to spread a little goodwill, I let him select a couple pastries and proceeded on my way to the place I call home.

Breakfasts tend to be simple affairs, mostly because Tina doesn't care for breakfast. Occasionally I'll fix Bea and I something more substantial. This morning we were having pastries, toast and jam, and a bracing Assam tea.

I was sitting at the dining room table, with a cup of hot tea and a cream cheese croissant, looking at the front page of the newspaper, when Bea joined me. She was wearing skinny leg jeans and a pale blue blouse, which was belted at the waist, flared out below the belt, and had puffed sleeves at the shoulder. Ever since she got advice from Solstice, Tina's renter, on how to buy clothes for her boyish figure, Bea's been looking knockout gorgeous. She kissed me good morning and sat next to me.

Before my little sweetheart could snare a doughnut, Tina joined us. My sister almost always wears a skirt suit and today was no exception. A pleated black skirt suit with white blouse, open at the throat, and a ruby necklace. Since she doesn't usually wear black, I assumed she was doing so in memoriam for our murdered client.

We exchanged greetings and fell into our usual breakfast routine: Bea and I sharing the paper, and Tina sticking her nose in her iPad.

About twenty minutes into breakfast, Tina suddenly asked, "Do you drink coffee, Bea?"

"Not really. I don't like it very much. Too bitter and burnt tasting. Once in a while I'll have a Latte macchiato or a Cappuccino. Mostly when I have coffee I just add lots of cream and sugar. Whipped cream is best."

Tina nodded and went back to her iPad.

Now you might think Tina's question odd. However, given Tina's almost maniacal hatred for anything even remotely smelling or tasting of coffee and that Cal made French Press coffee one morning for breakfast in our kitchen and that Tina threw a massive hissy fit over it and that Cal moved back home as a result and Tina is now regretting said hissy fit, I don't think the question at all odd.

When you have a Tina-sized ego, well, you'll fish for anything to justify your position that even motor oil is more potable than coffee.

On the other hand, if Bea had said she liked coffee then Tina would have been forced to consider the idea that her position is a mite inflexible and counterproductive to a long-term relationship with the man she loves.

Of course sleeping alone in your bed when not so long ago

said man shared it with you can be a powerful inducement to reconsider such a strongly held position, as well. Anyway, it's a thought. But then what do I know? Apart from Bea, my relationships with women have been less than stellar. About as successful as shifting gears when the clutch doesn't work.

We sat for a while longer. During which time Bea and I finished reading the paper, listened to Tina's insistence we wash our hands before we touch anything, and gave her our undying assurance we would.

I love my sister. She's the only family I have, but sometimes she is a great big pain in the ass. That I put up with her is because she's family and does have a heart of gold. It's just difficult to find said heart much of the time.

Tina finished her toast and orange marmalade, downed the remaining tea in her cup, stood, and announced she'd be in the music room. We no longer had a case so I said "okay". No need to push her to work when there was nothing to work on. Soon the dark tones of Arthur Foote's Suite Number 1 for piano sounded throughout the house. I just shook my head and cleaned up the dishes with Bea.

"Harry?"

"Bea?"

"Why doesn't Tina just apologize?"

"Why doesn't the Pope convert to animism?"

"It's so stupid. They love each other."

"I know."

She sighed. "I'll be at my desk. I have some paperwork to do."

"Do you still have Barlow's check?"

"I do. I didn't deposit it yet."

"Hang on to it. I need to decide how much of it is ours."

"Okay." She hugged me. "I love you so much, Harry."

I held her. "Thanks for throwing yourself at me, otherwise I would have missed out on the best thing to happen in my life."

"All I want is for Tina and Cal to be happy. Like we are."

"Hopefully in time, Babe. Hopefully in time."

She kissed me and went to the office. I poured myself a cup of tea and sat on one of the barstools. A notepad was on the counter. I got it and a pencil and began jotting numbers on the top sheet. I took a sip of tea and found myself wondering if the police had finally caught up with Celeste. Eventually they would. They'd want her to identify the body and they'd want a statement from her.

"I wonder what she does at that hotel?" My teacup said nothing and my mind drifted to places that didn't put the Reverend Mrs. Celeste Barlow in the best light. At least from a ministerial point of view. I finished my tea and went to the office, stopping at Bea's desk first.

"Go ahead and deposit the check, Babe. We'll need to return twelve grand to the Reverend's estate."

"Will do, my darling."

I kissed her, went on in to the Inner Sanctum, got seated at my desk, and Tina walked in.

"We can keep eight grand of the retainer," I announced.

"Good." She sat at her desk, took out a cigar, lit it, and poured herself a glass of madeira. "Do you think Celeste did it?"

I leaned back in my chair and put my hands behind my head. "Unknown. I suppose she could have left the hotel, gone home, carved him up, and returned."

Tina nodded and sighed. She puffed on the cigar and took a sip of wine. "So Jesus never wept."

"Come again?"

"If what Barlow said is true, that there never was a historical Jesus, that he's a myth like Paul Bunyan or Pecos Bill and not a legend like Davy Crockett or Daniel Boone, then Jesus wouldn't have wept."

I sat upright. "True. If he never existed, he couldn't have wept."

"And he never raised Lazarus, never said the Beatitudes, never talked to the woman at the well, or had that conversation with Nicodemus."

"Correct."

"Then who did Paul see on the Damascus Road?"

"Good question. Probably his own construct of what he thought Jesus was."

"He didn't see a vision?"

"He might of, but it was one his mind generated at a moment of emotional crisis. Or the entire story was made up to give Paul validity."

"By whom?"

"Anybody. Paul himself. One of his followers."

Tina thought a moment. "Therefore he was either seeing himself or it's all just a big lie."

"I suppose you could say that."

"Sure changes things if there was no Jesus. I wonder what Dad would've thought about this?"

I laughed. "He'd have shaken his head and muttered, 'heretics', then gone off to visit a church member or work on his sermon."

Tina smiled. "Yes. That's what he would have said or done."

A faraway look came over her face. Memories of days long gone. Days which no longer exist except in the mind, molded and fashioned into the stuff that makes us who we are. For good or for ill. Memories which bolster us or haunt us. Sweet dreams or nightmares.

"Harry, do you ever miss believing? Do you ever miss the faith?"

"No. It's a waste of time. If I want to follow something, there's stoicism. Quintessentially practical without all the folderol. It's what I used to tell my students."

"I know I was a great trial for Mother."

"Tell me about it. Every phone call and every letter. Her greatest fear was you'd end up pregnant."

Tina's voice got very quiet. "I know. It haunts me how I hurt her."

"She asked me to pray for you and I never had the courage to tell her I no longer believed."

"That's why I've always liked that verse, 'Jesus wept'. It gave me hope that maybe I could be forgiven."

"Forgiven? You were never a believer in the first place."

"I know. But, Harry, I've seen and done things that… Well, what if it's true? That there is a heaven and hell. I'd like to know I might be forgiven and if Jesus wept for Lazarus, well, maybe he might weep for me."

"I see your point. I don't think there is anything out there. And if there is, I find it difficult to believe it cares about us. Shoot, we get more empathy from Santa Claus. We have to care for ourselves and each other. Like you and me. We help each other."

She nodded. "It's kind of sad. That Jesus, the Son of God, could weep gave me hope he would understand me and maybe raise me from the dead. Now there is nothing."

"There always was nothing. I think you are feeling guilty for some reason. What you need to realize is the past is gone. Poof! It doesn't exist. There's no need for you to torture yourself over it. You can't change the past. All you can do is move on. Forgive yourself and move on."

Her steepled fingers were resting against her lips and her eyes were half-closed.

"Besides, Tina, you don't need anything out there. You have you. Love yourself. Love others. Be Jesus to yourself. You have me and Bea and if you'll let him, Cal. I love you, Sis. I'm here for you."

"Thanks. I love you, too, Big Brother. I'm glad you're here."

I got up from my desk and went to her. She stood and we hugged each other. Tina doesn't do much hugging. That was a special moment.

She pushed me away and with a smile said, "Don't you have work to do?"

"I guess you've had enough touchy-feely time for today."

"Oh, shut up."

"Yeah, like you mean it."

"What's for lunch?"

"I don't know, but I'm on it."

"Good." She picked up her book. No more emotion for today.

I looked through my recipes for something simple and comforting and decided on Baked Potato Soup.

"I'll be in the kitchen, if you need me."

Tina nodded.

I left the Inner Sanctum, kissed Bea, and walked to the kitchen where I worked my magic.

An hour later, soup simmering on the stove, I returned to the office. Bea was on the phone. I gave her a questioning look. She mouthed the words "my brother", I nodded, and told her to say "hi" for me.

On to the Inner Sanctum. Tina wasn't at her desk. She was sitting on the couch in front of the fire. I walked over and sat next to her. She was looking at a book. Without looking at me, she read out loud

> It matters not how strait the gate,
> How charged with punishments the scroll,
> I am the master of my fate:
> I am the captain of my soul.

"Truer words were never penned, Henley."

She smiled. "If he was right, then I'm the boss. Doesn't matter if there's a god or not, doesn't matter if Jesus wept or not. My fate is in my hands to do with as I see fit."

"Sums it up."

"You and Bea are happy?"

"Very."

"I love Cal."

"I know."

"Some days I wish I wasn't me."

"You are the mistress of your fate. Fix what you don't like."

She sighed. "Easier said than done."

"Not impossible. Just remember, the enemy is us."

"Okay, Mr. Doctor of Philosophy."

I kissed her cheek. "Gotta check the soup."

I left and went to the kitchen. Gave the pot a stir and almost tripped over Prudy, Tina's huge Maine Coon cat, who was getting ready to rub on my ankles.

From somewhere, Manly, Tina's big Manx, blazed through the kitchen with a yapping Buddy in hot pursuit. From the little glimpse I got, it looked like Manly had one of Buddy's toys in his mouth.

Tina's other cat, Isis, was probably under a blanket somewhere and in her own little warm paradise. She's one of those hairless Sphinx cats and in winter we rarely see her.

Prudy made another attempt to rub up against me. I picked her up, petted her, put her back down, washed my hands, and set the table.

After lunch, we returned to the office and sometime after two, Bea showed in Cal Swenson.

"Harry, Tina." He walked over to the oxblood oversized wing-back, which isn't oversized for him, and sat.

"And to what do we owe the honor of this visit?" Tina asked.

"Just stopped by to let you know, Celeste Barlow showed up at home this morning. How she slipped past Wilcox at the hotel puzzles me. Anyway, Nordquist broke the news to her and she followed him downtown to confirm the body belonged to her husband. Late husband. She gave us a statement. Very vague and when we started to press, she demanded her lawyer be present. We told her to go home but stay around, because we'd probably want to talk some more with her."

"What's your gut say?" Tina asked.

"Don't know. No alibi. Wasn't home. Won't say where she was, but I'd say her grief was genuine. So, I'm confused by this one. Nelson says she's guilty. Behaves like she's guilty. Thinks the tears are an act."

"Never met Celeste, Cal, so I can't say," Tina said.

He stood. "Well, I've work to do. Catch you later."

I walked him to the door and returned to the office.

"I'm going to work on supper."

Tina nodded and I left, stopping at Bea's desk. "You busy? Want to be my sous chef?"

"Sure!" She stood. "Let's go!"

We walked to the kitchen holding hands. I shooed Manly off the counter and wiped it down. Bea went to work making a salad. I prepared the T-Bones for broiling and made horseradish sauce. For the carb, I planned on baked potatoes. Pretty simple. But good food doesn't need to be complex. Kind of like life. Too often we make the simplest things a complex quagmire and then wonder why we're stuck.

3

FEINGOLD'S OFFER

Thursday morning, 6 February

THE DOORBELL RANG AT PRECISELY NINE-THIRTY. TINA WASN'T IN THE office. She was at the piano playing Beethoven's Fourth Piano Sonata. Bea and I were in the office sitting on the couch in front of the fire. And, yes, we were playing kissy face. When the doorbell rang, she went to answer the door and I moved to my desk. In a minute, she ushered in Harold Feingold. He and I shook hands and I invited him to take a seat. Bea indicated she'd get Tina.

We'd run into Feingold while investigating the Copley murder. He'd been Mrs. Copley's attorney and was impressed with Tina's performance in solving the case. So impressed, in fact, he hired her himself to work on a case for him a short time later. And now he was here again.

Tina entered and she and he exchanged greetings. She sat in her custom-made, ergonomically correct chair. He was seated in the oxblood oversized wingback at the far corner of Tina's desk.

He brushed something off the lapel of his Jay Kos suit. The piece of cloth probably set him back something over five grand. "This winter is simply intolerable. You look at the sky and it's a beautiful blue. Not a cloud up there. And the goddamn wind practically takes the flesh right off your bones. Twenty-four below windchill and five below for the actual temp. Makes me wonder why I didn't move to Florida or San Diego after law school."

Tina favored him with a smile. For the record, her Givenchy coat, skirt, blouse, and shoes set her back sixty-five hundred. "Living here ensures you won't have to move when the ice caps melt."

"They're melting in this winter? My God, I think penguins would pack up and move to the South Pole if they lived here. It has to be warmer there."

Tina shrugged. "That's what the greenies are saying."

He made a face. "I tell you, they're nuts. Crackpots. Cranks."

I chuckled to myself. Probably upset because they'd make him trade in his Beemer for a bicycle if they could.

Tina leaned back in her chair and crossed her legs. "I suppose it won't happen in our lifetime, so for us it's academic."

"I think you're right."

"I am." She had a twinkle in her eye and added, "Or at least a Wright."

Feingold smiled. "Good one. But we can talk about the environment all day and not solve anything. Whereas we have a much easier problem at hand, which is solvable."

"We do?" Tina's tone of voice indicated she didn't believe it.

"Yes, we do. That of Celeste Barlow. The Reverend Celeste Barlow."

Tina cast me a sidelong glance. I smiled and she said, "Indeed. And what problem does the Reverend Celeste Barlow have?"

"The police have her as the chief suspect in the murder of her husband."

"Have they arrested her?"

"Not yet."

"You don't think she did it?"

"Doesn't matter what I think. She hired me to make her a non-suspect, which is why I'm here."

"What if she did it?"

"Then we find some technicality on which to get her off."

"And what do you want me to do?"

"Find out who did it. And if she did, then find out where the police screwed up."

We no longer had Celeste's husband for a client. Therefore no conflict of interest on our part. At least on that particular front. Where conflict might lie was in the arena of Tina's relationship with Cal. If she took the case it could put them at odds. Something their relationship didn't exactly need right now.

Tina didn't say anything. My guess? She was analyzing the possible damage accepting the case might cause her already tenuous relationship with Cal. Feingold, however, apparently thought the silence had to do with money and Tina's antipathy towards work.

"Look, Miss Wright, I know your proclivity for not taking cases. So let's cut to the chase. Two thousand an hour, plus expenses, and a fifty thousand dollar non-refundable retainer."

Tina looked at me. I shrugged and nodded. To Feingold she said, "You're throwing a lot of money at me. Why?"

"Because I think it will move you and because the police are fairly certain they have their perp. And you know how they are when they think everything is all neat and tidy — they don't look for anything else. Just stuff that will reinforce their pre-conceived neat and tidy solution."

"Why focus so early on Mrs. Barlow?"

"She's not giving them anything. No alibi. No information. Nothing. Like she wants to fall on her sword. Two years ago, she and the deceased had a big fight in their driveway at two in the morning and she threatened to kill him. And you know the police. She's convenient and they like convenient."

"An argument in the driveway is hardly indicative of anything. Spouses threaten to kill each other all the time and never do."

"True. But Barlow is dead and his wife is not presenting an

alibi and is being vague about her whereabouts to boot. And that makes her convenient."

"Does she know seppuku? Or have any Japanese connections?"

"Not that I know of, but she's not telling me shit either."

Tina closed her eyes and rested her chin on steepled fingers.

After half a minute she opened them. "The fifty K is mine even if hours and expenses don't add up to fifty."

"Correct. And if they go over, you get more."

"Okay, Mr. Feingold, I'll take the case. Harry, give Mr. Feingold a contract."

I gave him a contract and he pulled out of his suit coat pocket a check for fifty grand. He signed the contract and gave me both pieces of paper. I signed the contract, made a copy, and gave the copy to him.

He stood. "I'll bring the Reverend Mrs. Barlow tomorrow and you can talk to her. Maybe you'll get somewhere with her."

"Very good. Give the time to Bea when you have it, will you?" Tina said.

"I'll have Lolana call. A pleasure, Miss Wright."

"Likewise," Tina replied.

Feingold left and Tina and I looked at each other.

I was shaking my head. "What are the odds of that happening?"

"About the same as Jesus having wept."

4

BY EDICT OF THE EMPEROR

Thursday afternoon into evening, 6 February

FOR LUNCH, I WHIPPED UP A VARIETY OF TEA SANDWICHES AND HORS d'oeuvres. Cucumber, deviled egg, sweet onion, and roasted vegetables with goat cheese sandwiches. The hors d'oeuvres were Tuna Nicoise Crostinis, Taleggio Flatbread, Caramelized Onion Tartlets, and Endive Boats with Marinated Vegetables. To accompany our little sandwiches and starters, I opened a bottle of California Gewürztraminer and one of Missouri Cayuga.

When the food was ready I announced lunch and Bea and Tina joined me in the dining room. When the women entered, Bea was saying, "...made it all sound like it really happened." They sat and Bea asked, "Is that true, Harry, the Bible is a lie?"

I took a sip of Cayuga and a bite of a cucumber sandwich, mostly so I had time to think. I chewed and swallowed. "I don't think the Bible is a lie, but it's not *The Truth* either. It just is. You have to understand it in the context in which it was written, why it was written, and the form in which it was written. It's not history as we understand history today. The fundagelicals want to believe it is a true and accurate history, but form alone argues against that belief."

"So why does the church teach the Bible is a history book and Jesus is the Savior?" Bea's puzzlement showed on her face, until she bit into an Endive Boat. Her expression hinted she was open to believing the Endive Boat was *The Truth.*

"Mostly force of habit." I drank wine and ate a Caramelized Onion Tartlet.

"I don't get it." More puzzlement and more Endive Boat.

I leaned back in my chair, a sweet onion sandwich in one hand. "On February 27, 380, Nicene Christianity became the official religion of the Roman Empire. In one imperial edict paganism and Arian Christianity were outlawed. Today's Christianity was established by edict. Not proof. And for over sixteen centuries that's how it's been. It was only in the nineteenth century that we see religion and state begin to separate and its only been in the past sixty years that the cultural majority in the west has moved beyond Christianity.

"So force of habit set in motion by an imperial edict is mostly why we believe in a historical Jesus. Otherwise there is no proof for his existence. To cite the New Testament as proof of Jesus's historicity, besides being a logical fallacy, is akin to citing the Book of Mormon as proof of an ancient Nephite civilization in America. There is no outside corroboration of the existence of either."

"Wow, Harry, that's heavy stuff." Bea took a bite out of a flatbread.

"It's only heavy if you're invested in the belief either collection of books is the truth. Otherwise, they have no impact."

A thoughtful look settled on Bea's face. "What you're saying, my love, is that the New Testament can't be used to prove Jesus existed, just like a Batman comic book can't be used as proof Batman exists. Because outside of the comic books, there is no proof for Batman and Robin."

"That's what I'm saying."

Tina added, "Therefore, Jesus didn't weep for Lazarus and he doesn't weep for us."

"Because he's just a figment of someone's imagination," Bea concluded.

"Basically." I took a sip of wine and thought, huh, wine and bread, sort of a last communion.

"Wow." Bea shook her head and picked up a deviled egg sandwich. "Can I still get you a Christmas present?"

"Sure," I replied.

"Don't forget me."

"Of course I wouldn't forget you, Tina, you're the reason I'm here and Mrs. Wright."

A smirk appeared on Tina's face. "You got that right."

"And I am right," Bea said and laughed.

When I didn't say anything, they looked at me and chorused, "Harry?"

"Yeah, yeah, I'm right, too. Sheesh."

———

After lunch, Bea and I cleaned up the dining room and kitchen. When finished, Bea went back to her post and I made a pot of tea, which I brought into the office. The temp had warmed up to a sultry two above zero. The wind, however, was rattling the windows and making it feel like it was seventeen below. I think Feingold had a point.

Tina was at her desk smoking a cigar and had poured a glass of madeira. I poured myself a cup of tea. Bea had declined my offer.

"Why the hell did you move from San Francisco to Minneapolis?"

Tina put down her book. "What's wrong with Minneapolis?"

"Too damn cold here."

"It does get cold. It also gets hot and muggy in the summer and all the lakes are breeding grounds for a zillion mosquitoes. I didn't come here because of the weather. Every place has its problems. I came here because it is the Midwest and we grew up in the

Midwest. I came here because I liked the multi-cultural nature of what is in essence a small city. I have what I grew up with and I have something of what I liked about San Francisco. Minneapolis and St Paul have a little bit of everything. And I like that. They are conservative and liberal all at the same time."

The phone rang and Bea answered. A minute later she poked her head into the Inner Sanctum and told us the call was from Lolana. Feingold and Celeste Barlow would be at our place at eleven o'clock.

Tina puffed on the cigar. "Harry, call Feingold and ask him if Celeste is at home."

I picked up my desk phone, dialed Feingold's number, asked Lolana when she answered if her boss was in. She said he was and put me through to him, and in a minute I was asking Tina's question.

"No, she's not at the house and she won't tell me where she is staying. I just have the house number, which must roll over to her cell."

"Okay. Thanks." I hung up and relayed the info to the boss.

She thought a minute, then said, "Her own attorney doesn't even know where she is." She shook her head. "Call Ed and see if he's available. I want you and him to watch the Barlow house. We need to know when the little birdie flies back to the nest."

"Even with her coming here tomorrow?"

"Yes. Damn odd behavior on her part. Don't you think?"

"I do." I picked up the phone to call Ed Hafner, one of the three freelancers Tina uses to gather information for her. He answered on the fourth ring. After exchanging greetings, I told him what Tina wanted.

"Yeah, I'm free. I can do it."

"Great. I'll take the graveyard shift so the Missus doesn't get mad at us."

"That's awfully considerate of you, Harry."

"Yep. All around Mr. Nice Guy, I am." I gave him the address and told him to get there ASAP. He said he would and we hung up.

Bea poked her head in. "Hey, guys, I'm going to the bank to deposit checks. Need anything while I'm out?"

Tina and I both indicated there was nothing pressing we needed. Bea crossed over to my desk, gave me a kiss, and left on her errand.

"When are you going to tell Cal?"

"Don't know. Not today."

"Okay. I'm going to get supper started."

She nodded and I departed for the kitchen. Cabbage jambalaya was on the menu. I fired up the iPod and listened to Beethoven string quartets while preparing our supper. When she got back, Bea joined me and asked if I needed help. I told her no, but she was welcome to keep me company.

"Have to work tonight, Babe," I said. "Want to come along?"

"What are we doing?"

I like that about Bea. She just dives right in. "We're going to do a stakeout to see if Celeste Barlow shows up on her own doorstep any time before she shows up here."

"Does that mean we can snuggle in the back seat?"

"Maybe."

"Okay. I'll bring blankets and a thermos of tea."

"Some munchies, too."

"I'm not going to be enough for you?"

"You're kind of small."

"I may be small but I'll satisfy all your desires and you won't even think about munchies."

"We do have to watch the house, you know."

"We'll work it out."

Her grin made her look like a succubus in heat.

5

BUSINESS WOMAN

Friday 11am to noon, 7 February

FEINGOLD ARRIVED RIGHT ON THE DOT AT ELEVEN. CELESTE WAS FOUR minutes late. She didn't give a reason. I rather like that. Displays a certain confidence and an "I don't care what you think" attitude.

Celeste Barlow looked younger than her forty-five years. Her brown hair, which fell past her shoulders, had luscious body and a curl to the ends. If I were a betting man, I'd wager a portion of the loveliness of her hair came from some product contained in a bottle. But it didn't look it. She was a very attractive woman and made judicious use of makeup to enhance what God, if he exists, gave her. Her eyes were dark and I'd guess the color to be a dark brown.

She was wearing a deep burgundy jumpsuit, with very wide flair legs, which made the outfit look like a dress. The top had a rounded neckline and the wide sleeves were elbow length. The back of the outfit's top was nothing more than an X of fabric. It was clear, at least to these eyes, she jiggled too much to be wearing a bra. Her shoes were stiletto heels and the color matched her outfit. On her head was a wool beret-style beanie hat with a bow. The hat and bow were in the same deep burgundy as her outfit. She wore a long, waist-length strand of pearls. In her left hand was a burgundy clutch. I didn't get to see her winter coat, she having left it with Bea.

Feingold had taken the oversized wingback, so I positioned the Reverend on the end of the chesterfield closest to me. Might as well take in the eye candy while I had the chance. I introduced Tina and myself to the Reverend, Bea having announced her when she entered. I didn't mention Feingold. I assumed she knew her attorney.

Once seated, the Reverend Celeste Barlow and Tina looked at each other for close to a minute. Some form of communication must've been passing between the two. Finally Tina spoke, "Mr. Feingold, would you step out into the waiting area and have a seat there?"

"Miss Wright, I should—"

Celeste cut him off. "Just do it, Harold."

"Very well," he muttered, got up, and left.

"You want me to go?" I asked.

"You can stay," Celeste said. "She'll probably tell you anyway."

"So what is it you do, Mrs. Barlow?" Tina asked.

"You already know, but if you want to hear me say it, I'm a whore. High class. But a whore nonetheless."

"Are you ashamed of what you do?"

Celeste paused before speaking. "No, I wouldn't say ashamed. Old habits and old ways of thinking, though, die hard."

"That they do. You run a fair and honest business?"

"I do. My clients get their money's worth."

"Then let the old stuff die."

Celeste smiled. "Easier said than done. I can't exactly tell my mother or children I'm a hooker."

"True. The Victorian mindset is still alive and further complicated by Hollywood's romanticization of love."

Celeste laughed. "Yes, Victoria still holds on to us from the grave. But don't you love someone?"

"I do. However things were easier when it was just sex."

Celeste nodded. "Ah, yes. There is that."

"Did your husband know?"

"I don't think so. He knew something was different, something had changed, and I don't think he liked it. The change, that is." Her lower lip started quivering. "I didn't think he'd understand." Her lip was going to town and I thought she was going to break down, but she got herself under control, took a deep breath, and went on. "And no, I didn't kill him. I loved him."

Tina nodded. "You wouldn't be the first person, however, who killed the person she loved. Any ideas who might have wanted him dead?"

"No."

"Why are you keeping this from Feingold?"

"Lawyers. They're like gossipy tenth grade girls. I have some very important people who rely on my discretion."

"Yet you trust Harry and me."

"You're business people."

Tina smiled. "We are. What can you tell me about your husband?"

"I met him in seminary."

"Where?"

"Harvard Divinity School."

"Okay. Go on."

"We married when I graduated. I was two years behind him. That was in '94 when we were married. Our son was born a year later and our daughter three years after him. Gary was a good husband and father. He was devoted to his congregation. He was a man of faith."

"Yet someone killed him and did so in a horrific manner."

Celeste nodded and started crying. She pulled a tissue out of her clutch and dabbed her eyes.

"The police see you as a prime suspect because you won't tell them who you were with the night your husband was killed. Why?"

"Because I was entertaining the Minnesota Secretary of State and his wife."

"I see. Other than a customer, is the Secretary or his wife anything to you?"

"No."

"You'd rather go to prison than betray a customer's confidence."

"Priests have privilege. Lawyers have privilege. Why shouldn't prostitutes?"

"You won't get an argument out of me, but is the confidence worth going to prison over?"

"That's why Feingold wanted to hire you. To find who killed my husband so I don't need to say anything and can keep my secret life secret."

"You aren't giving me much to work with. What do you know of your husband before you met him?"

"Let's see. He was born in 1966. Graduated from high school in 1984 and college in 1988. He was a philosophy major in college. Attended seminary from 1989 to 1992."

"What did he do between college and seminary?"

Celeste leaned back, her head elevated slightly in thought. Finally, she said, "I don't really know. All he said is he travelled, but was never specific about where he went or what he did. I think that was a time in his life he wasn't very proud of. Perhaps even ashamed. Why else would he not want to talk about it? You see, even though Gary was quite liberal in his theology, he was a devote man. Almost like a monk. I think he would have made a good one, except he was very social."

Now it was Tina's turn. She leaned back in her chair, steepled fingers touching her chin, and closed her eyes. After a couple minutes she leaned forward and asked, "Reverend Barlow, why did you go into the sex trade?"

Celeste smiled, but the smile was a bitter one. "With every client I'm telling the church and society, 'Fuck you'."

"Why do you want to tell them that?"

"The lies. The repression and suppression of women. Even my very liberal denomination is run by the old boys's club. Women get the shit churches."

"Many see prostitution as demeaning to women."

"Do you?" Celeste shot back.

"No. I don't. It's a job like any other. Men and women like sex and are often willing to pay to get it. Why shouldn't other men and women sell what they have and others want?"

Celeste smiled. "I agree with you. But our Victorian mores don't. So by being an escort. I can show my disdain for the church and its lies and society's antiquated mores and have fun at the same time. I'm an actress, a therapist, a provider of pleasure — all rolled into one."

"Do you enjoy the sex?"

"Very often. It's more fun when it's illegal," Celeste said with a laugh.

"May I ask what you charge?" I asked.

"If you have to ask, you probably can't afford me." Celeste favored me with a smile and an appraising look. "I'm an escort. Minimum time to rent my services is two hours. An escort who offers half-hour or hourly rates is escorting you from the door to the bed and that's it. I'm upscale. Dinner, dancing, concerts, theater, and the like. A man rents me to be his companion for an occasion. If we have sex, well…" She shrugged. "One thousand dollars for the two hours. For dinner and the evening, four thousand. One night, eight thousand. A weekend is fifteen thousand. Other time periods are negotiable. Money upfront. Cash only. Small bills preferred."

I looked at her. She was indeed very attractive. I could see where a man would want her on his arm for the evening. I said, "I can afford your rates. I was just curious, though. I'm happily married and won't be needing your services. However, I now know what my wife can charge." The last I said with a big smile.

Celeste chuckled. "You going into pimping?"

I shrugged. "Sometimes we have slow days."

Celeste laughed. "I'd like to meet your wife and get her reaction to what you just said."

"You met her. She's our receptionist."

Celeste arched an eyebrow.

Tina had apparently found my conversation with Celeste amusing. She added, "If any man I know kissed like Bea, I'd have married him yesterday."

Celeste raised both her eyebrows and looked at Tina, who nodded. Celeste turned back to me. Her face looked thoughtful. "Maybe we can make a business arrangement. I'll give you my card." She reached into her clutch and withdrew a business card, which I retrieved from her.

Tina returned us to the interview. "Your husband had no enemies, I take it."

"Other than church people, I'm not aware of any. Certainly none who would want to kill him."

"You have any disgruntled clients?"

"On occasion. Not many, though. How would that involve Gary?"

"Don't know. Get back at you, perhaps."

"But how could they find him? I don't use my real name."

"All they need is a photo and Google can do the rest."

"I see. Hadn't thought of that. Privacy is an illusion in our modern world, isn't it?"

Tina nodded.

"Just like the church," Celeste said softly.

"Are you always at The Hotel Minneapolis?"

"How do you know I have a room there?"

"Your husband hired me to follow you and find out what you were up to."

"I'm not surprised. He didn't say much, but I knew my mysterious activities were bothering him. I'm glad he didn't find out. He was very disappointed I left the ministry and then the church. He couldn't understand if there never was a Jesus, it's all just a lie. One can still follow the Golden Rule and not put up with the politics of the church. But he saw value in ritual. He thought more than doctrine, it is the ritual of the church that comforts people. And maybe he was right."

"Where else do you hang out your shingle, so to speak?"

"The Ivy. The Hilton, Even the W on occasion. Very often I go to where my client is staying. Once in a while I go out of town. Convention. Ski holiday. But usually I'm here."

"I assume your children are coming home?"

"Yes. They're arriving tomorrow. I'll be returning to the house then."

"Where are they?" Of course Tina was only asking this pro forma. We already knew where they were.

"They're at Groton-Peabody Academy in Massachusetts."

"Do you get your husband's money?"

"Yes. He, his estate, is worth eight to ten million. I'm worth four to five. Depends on where the markets are at."

Tina nodded, however I interrupted before she continued with her next question. "If you have all that money, why go into the escort business?"

Celeste chuckled. "Let me ask you this: who ever has enough money that they don't want more?"

"You're asking the wrong person. I'm not money motivated."

"Really? How very interesting. We'll have to talk about that sometime. Well, I like money. I used to feel guilty about it when I was a minister. Just another tool of the church to make you feel guilty. I'm tired of feeling guilty. I like money and being an escort is easy money and I make quite a lot of it."

I gave Tina a look indicating I was finished.

Tina began, "Reverend—"

"Please. Call me 'Celeste'. The Reverend bit is in the past and I'd like to keep it there."

"Very well, Celeste, for now I think I'm done. But I may wish to talk to you further. How may I reach you?"

"Call my home phone." She then recited the number and I jotted it down.

She stood and we did as well. She walked up to Tina's desk and extended her hand, which Tina took. "Thank you, Justinia. Please find who did this."

"I'll do my best."

Celeste nodded, turned around, and walked to the door. I was there to open it for her.

"Remember my offer," she said.

I winked and she walked into the outer office and looked at Bea. She turned to me and gave me a nod. Then she turned to Feingold. "Let's get lunch, Harold, I'm starving." And they left, but not before he helped her with her floor length fur coat.

"Why did she look at me like that?" Bea asked after they were gone.

"Business."

"Business?"

"Yeah. You had to be there."

"Oh."

Bea's hair was curled and she was wearing makeup. The bright red lipstick giving her face lots of color. Her dress had puff sleeves at the shoulder, was belted at the waist, and the full skirt ended at the knees. The color was a light blue. She looked delicious.

"Lunch sounds like a good idea," I said.

"I'm starving. I put a tuna bake in the oven. Is that okay?"

"Fine with me. I'll get the boss."

I went back into the Inner Sanctum. "You want lunch?"

"Yes. I can't believe she's willing to go to prison to save some politician and his wife's reputations. I wonder what the connection is?"

"Don't know. She didn't give us much."

"No, she didn't."

"We're left with something in his past or her past—"

"Or present."

"Or present. Possibly something in the children's lives. Or a random murder."

Tina stood. "That about sums it up. Although I think we can scratch the random murder. No one randomly murders by seppuku."

"You have a point."

"Which means, someone wanted him dead."

6

FALL FROM GRACE

Friday afternoon, 7 February

AFTER LUNCH, BEA WAS AT HER DESK IN THE OUTER OFFICE, TINA AND I were at our desks in the inner office.

I was smoking my pipe and having tea. Tina was smoking a cigar and also having tea. Why tea instead of her usual madeira was beyond me. When I asked her, she simply said because she wanted to. It might have been that the windchill was still below zero. Two days in a row of this crap gets to be a bit much.

"So where do we begin, O Great Detective?"

"Harry, sometimes you are very annoying."

"Yep."

"For starters, tell Ed to go home."

I made the call. Ed was glad. With the temp as cold as it was outside, sitting in a car is not all that fun. Unless you have Bea with you. I turned to Tina. "Now what?"

"Call the Secretary of State's office."

"You want me to call Matt Rhinelander?"

"Sure. He's not John Kerry."

"Okay. I'll see what I can do."

I spent over two hours on the phone. In the end, his people weren't going to work with us.

"No luck. Next time we donate lots of money to the Democrats. Hell. While we're at it, might as well throw money at the Republicans too. That way we'll have all the bases covered. And being big contributors, then they'll have to talk to us."

"Did you take a look at Celeste's blog?"

I shook my head. "No. Why?"

"I did, while you were on the phone. Very interesting. She's really bent out of shape over Jesus never existing."

"Seems to me it's about time to let it go and move on."

"One would think so. It's been years now and she is still going on about the evil deception the church pulls on people."

"Any intimations about her new career?"

"No. Nothing overly personal on the blog."

"Does she get a lot of visitors?"

"Don't know. No counter."

"Was it difficult to find?"

"Not really. Have you looked at her business card?"

"No."

"You waiting for Christmas?"

I shook my head. A regular slave driver. Sheesh. I picked up the card. Plain white with black letters. The letters spelled out Sunny Day, Gentleman's Escort. In the lower left corner was her email address and in the lower right was a website URL: Sunny-DayandFriends.com.

I tapped the keys on my computer keyboard and, voilà, the entry page appeared. I was given the choice of entering my username and password or registering. Since I didn't have a username and password, I registered.

Once inside the site, there wasn't much to see. I could take a tour or sign-up for one of several different escort package levels. Or I could view the video and picture gallery.

To sign up, I had to pay a thousand dollar application fee and be vetted. Only after my membership was approved would I then be able to choose my membership level. I decided to take the tour.

"I'm going to take the tour of Sunny Day's little online whore-house. Want to watch the tour with me?"

Tina came over to my desk and sat on a corner. I clicked on the play button for the tour and the video started rolling. A seductive voice began telling me all about Sunny Day and her Friends. I'm not a prude, yet I found myself wondering how a minister could put something like that out on the web. Tour over, I then wandered through the picture gallery, Tina looking over my shoulder. After sampling the eye candy, we watched a short movie, one of three in the picture gallery. And that was some movie.

Tina's response was, "Holy shit. That is one hell of a long fall from grace." She paused for a moment before continuing, "So a person pays the application fee and goes through a vetting process."

"Probably she wants to be sure the guy has bucks."

Tina nodded her agreement. "Once the membership has been approved, then the person gets to sign up for one of four levels. Base membership gives you some pics and vids and the ability to rent an escort. The Silver level gives you the Base and one free evening per year with an escort. The Gold, gives you the Base plus a free night with an escort and two twenty percent off coupons for dinner and an evening. The Platinum level, at a one-time twenty-five thousand dollar fee gives you half-price services for life. Wow."

"And considering the Silver and Gold memberships are three hundred and fifty and twelve hundred and fifty respectively, we're talking a lot of money coming in just in the monthly fees."

"She is indeed rolling in the dough."

"I know people are willing to pay for sex. I just never thought folks would want sex this badly to pay such high prices for it."

"Harry, sometimes you are naive. You see those women? None of them are dogs. They are all very good looking. Rich and powerful men like to have a good looking woman on their arm and, if they are older, they especially like a young and good looking woman on their arm. It shows the youngsters they still have what it takes."

"Bah. It just takes money."

Tina shrugged. "So? The whole thing is a game. A play. It is all illusion. Smoke and mirrors. You, of all people, should know this. Isn't it what you are always telling me? The world is just illusion?"

"It is and I see where you are going."

"So there. However, am I reading this right? There are branch offices?"

I nodded. "That's what it looks like. Minneapolis, Chicago, Des Moines, St Louis, Dallas, Phoenix, San Diego, Seattle, Cleveland, and Boston. She has a very large swath of territory covered. I wonder who her girls are?"

"That would be interesting to find out. Relatives? Friends? Strangers?"

I chuckled. "Maybe she's running the Amway of bordellos."

"Whatever it is, it is a very enterprising fall from grace." Tina returned to her desk. "Well, Big Brother, you interested in signing up? Spice up your love life?"

"I have Bea. I don't need any spice. Bea keeps me quite busy and satisfied, thank you. Besides, she's pretty damn spicy as it is."

There was a smirk on her face. "If you say so."

"I do. Wouldn't think it to look at her. It's that old saying, don't judge a book by its cover."

"Although of late, she is looking pretty hot. Emma Watson, move over."

I agreed. "Ain't that the truth. In the end, I don't think the website provided us with anything useful."

"Not at the moment. We still need to either find the murderer or come up with an alibi for Celeste. Although the site asked for a lot of personal information. I wonder…" She poured a glass of madeira and lit a fresh cigar.

My pipe was out and I set it aside. I poured myself a fresh cup of tea. "What do you wonder?"

"Maybe the vetting gives her something else."

"Like what?"

"Financial information so she can extort more money out of the men."

"That would be an even bigger fall from grace."

Tina blew out a cloud of smoke. "It would, wouldn't it? I wonder if she runs all this herself. It seems like a huge time suck maintaining all this. How would she have time to entertain any men herself?"

"Good question. Maybe she has a manager."

"Hm. Given the scope of her enterprise and her own personal involvement in the service end, I would think she'd have to."

Tina closed her eyes and I watched her puff on the Muniemaker Long for several minutes. I timed her. Finally she spoke.

"To come up with an alibi we need to establish she was not at the house when her husband was murdered. We're not positive she didn't go home and kill him, but it seems unlikely. Second, we need to establish she didn't hire anyone to kill him. Check with the neighbors tomorrow, Harry, and find out if anyone saw anything. We'll start there."

"Are we going to look at who the murderer might be?"

"Not right now. The police are doing that and I don't want to be stepping on toes. They get a little testy when they find a private dick crossing over into their turf. We'll stick to the alibi angle for now. I know it isn't what Feingold hired us to do, but if it gets his client off the hook what would he care? Although I keep coming back to the question, why seppuku? And thus far I have no answer. Though if I can answer that question, I will have a very good idea of who killed the Reverend Gary Barlow, which would make both Feingold and the police very happy."

7

CAL VISITS

Friday night, 7 February

WHILE I WAS CONSIDERING TINA'S COMMENT ABOUT SEPPUKU, SHE excused herself and left the office. I looked at the clock and decided I'd better get at it if we were going to eat supper tonight. I went to the kitchen and took my sous chef with me.

"What are you making, Harry?"

"Porcini Parmesan."

"What else are we going to have?"

"A winter salad of delicata squash, gem lettuce, endive, and avocado."

"Sounds yummy."

"Good. Because you're going to make the salad."

"Okay."

"The recipe is there." And I pointed to it.

We made supper and when the Porcini Parmesan was in the oven, we moved to the game room and played pool. Bea skunked me three games to zip. At six-thirty I took the casserole out of the oven and was uncorking a bottle of Alexis Bailly Frontenac when the doorbell rang.

"I'll get it." Bea gave me a peck on the cheek and went to the front door.

A moment later I heard a squeal of delight and then there was Bea dragging Lieutenant Cal Swenson into the kitchen.

"Look who I found on our doorstep!"

"Hey, Cal!"

"Major. The Red Baron home?"

"She is. Playing the piano."

He nodded.

"Go on," I said.

He walked to the music room, while Bea and I transferred casserole, salad, and wine to the dining room.

"I hope he stays for supper," Bea said.

"It would be rather nice. Like old times."

"Yeah."

Tina and Cal walked into the dining room arm in arm. "Is there enough for Cal?" she asked.

"You betcha," I answered.

"Okay, I'll stay," he said.

Bea grabbed another plate and set of flatware and put them on the table for our man in blue.

"How's my beer buddy?" he asked Bea.

She giggled. "I'm fine."

"Glad to hear it."

We sat down. Bea passed Cal the main dish.

He looked at the casserole, looked at me, and said, "What is it?"

"Porcini Parmesan. Like Eggplant Parmesan only with mushrooms instead of eggplant."

He nodded, dished some up, and passed the dish to Tina. The salad came next and he took some of that.

"Wine, Cal?" I asked.

He looked at Bea. "What are you drinking?"

"I was going to have a little wine."

"Huh. Gone over to the dark side, I see."

"No, not really. It just goes good with this."

"Uh-huh. Okay, Harry, I'll have some wine."

I poured him a glass of Frontenac and passed the bottle around.

"So, Sweet Cheeks," Tina began and a hint of a smile appeared on Cal's face, "was there a Jesus or is he only a myth, like Paul Bunyan?"

"What?" His face was a mask of puzzlement.

Tina repeated the question.

"Does it matter?

And that discussion occupied us through the meal. When we'd finished eating, I announced, "We have Alexis Bailly Ratafia over vanilla ice cream with chocolate curls for dessert. Anyone interested?"

Everyone was game, so I made four bowls and we concluded our meal in the living room. When finished, while Bea was collecting the bowls, Cal said, "I stopped by to let you know it looks like the County Attorney is getting ready to charge Celeste Barlow with the murder of her husband. Just letting you know, since he was your client and you found the body and all."

"Thanks," Tina said and then asked, "What evidence indicates she did it?"

"She has no alibi and is evasive concerning her whereabouts. She bought the katana and tanto for her husband last year. Her fingerprints were on the tanto and traces of his blood. He hired you to investigate her because she is living some kind of double life. The county attorney figures she has a boyfriend she's protecting for some reason and maybe they worked together. Also, she and her husband had a big fight a couple of years ago and she threatened to kill him."

"Have you found the alleged boyfriend?" Tina asked.

"No."

"The fingerprints could have been there from when she gave him the weapons," Tina added.

"True."

"The case seems weak. What's the rush?"

"Don't know."

Tina took a deep breath. "Cal, you should know Harold Feingold hired me to find Gary Barlow's murderer or establish an alibi for Celeste."

His face took on a perturbed look. "Now why doesn't that surprise me? Dueling partners again."

"Just because Celeste's attorney—"

"You know how this works, Buttercup. We can't be together and we shouldn't be talking to each other. Even like right now. We are on opposite sides and when that happens, you…" He cleared his throat. "I'm looking for evidence to convict her and you're looking for evidence to get her off the hook. Not quite the same thing."

Tina didn't pick up on the broken off "you". She didn't have to. She and I knew where Cal decided not to go. Tina does things her way and lots of times it isn't the police way.

They've had numerous arguments over "method". The Alicia Harris case, which resulted in Bea and I meeting, is a case in point and a recent one. Tina's talk with the suspect led to him committing suicide. Cal was royally pissed over that one. Didn't see or talk to her for over six months.

Now, when they might be able to iron out issues, they are once again on opposite sides. And when that happens, well, it isn't necessarily good for their relationship.

"I know, Cal," Tina said, "but we want the same thing. Don't we? To get who really killed Barlow."

Bea's face was crestfallen. She was coming to the realization Tina and Cal weren't going to be together until the case was over.

"I suppose you don't think she did it."

"No, I don't."

He shook his head. He suddenly looked weary. "You talk to her?"

"Today."

"She have an alibi?"

Tina nodded.

"Jesus H. Christ. So why isn't she using it?"

"Don't know. Haven't figured out that angle yet."

"So you're saying we need to keep looking."

"Yes. I think there is something in Barlow's past, but maybe one of the other family member's past which is the cause. Find that and we find the killer."

Cal nodded. "However, until the county attorney is of a different opinion I have to find evidence to show she did it."

"But if there isn't any...?" Bea let the question hang in the air.

"Then we won't find any and it's back to square one," Cal finished. He wiped his hand over his face. "And until that point, we can't be together."

Tina's voice was soft. "I suppose so."

"No supposing about it. I best get going. Thanks, Major, for the meal. Top drawer as usual, although I wish you'd serve meat on occasion."

"Thanks, Cal, and I do. You need to visit more often."

"I'll keep that in mind."

Tina walked Cal to the door and when she returned, Bea was ready.

"Is Cal coming back here to live?"

"No. At least not yet." There was a touch of sadness in Tina's voice. "I did tell him he could have coffee here, as long as he supplied it, made it, and did the clean up."

I was flabbergasted. "Well, wonders never cease. Good thing I was sitting down."

Tina stuck out her tongue at me. Bea was jumping up and down like a little girl.

"I'm so glad," she squealed.

"Unfortunately, since we're working on opposite sides of this case, we can't see or talk to each other."

Bea was persistent. "But when it's over, then he can?"

"Yes, then he can. Although he said he wants to take this slow. Doesn't want to be a yo-yo, here one day and gone the next. So we'll see each other and maybe he'll be here on weekends. We'll see."

"It's a start," Bea said, a great big smile on her face. "Oh, boy, I'm so excited!"

"Not half as excited as I am," Tina replied.

8

THE DIGGING BEGINS IN EARNEST

Saturday, 8 February

The three of us were at breakfast, Tina, Bea, and I.

As usual, Buddy was curled up under Bea's chair, Manly was poking him trying to get a rise out of him, Prudy was sitting in Tina's lap, Isis was probably under a blanket somewhere, and Bea and I were reading the newspaper, which we'd just gotten back to after enduring Tina's harangue about germs and printer's ink getting on our hands and everything we touched.

She stopped and returned her nose to her iPad when we promised we'd wash our hands. Perhaps you can see why she and Cal have trouble staying together. She can be damned near impossible to live with at times. One of these days I'm going to have to ask her if Dad beat her with the paper when she was a kid or was it some Russian spy.

We maintained that tableau for a good twenty to twenty-five minutes, when Tina suddenly said, "I want all three here, pronto."

I got out my cell and told it to call "David". He answered on the third ring, I told him he was wanted, he said it was nice to be wanted, and would be at our place ASAP. We disconnected and I told the phone to call "Gwen". She picked up right away. I told her she was being summoned, she laughed, and said she was on her way. I repeated the process for Ed Hafner. Unfortunately, he was working. He thought he'd be free tomorrow and I told him I'd call back if he was still needed.

Tina stood and said she'd be in the office. "And don't forget to wash your hands." She did have to get that in before she left. Sheesh.

Bea and I cleaned up the dishes and put the leftovers away. When the dishwasher was running, I poured myself a cup of tea and Bea and I went to work. She took up her position at her desk in the outer office. I gave her a kiss and proceeded to my desk in the Inner Sanctum. Tina was sitting at her desk, looking at something on the computer.

I sat at my desk. "Do you want me to check out the neighbors now or wait until after the gang arrives?"

"Go later. I want you to start digging into Celeste's past. From the day she was conceived to the present."

"Okay. I'm on it."

The doorbell rang and in a moment Bea showed in David Nagasawa. We exchanged good mornings and the doorbell rang again. David's the best freelance operative this side of the North Pole. Bea showed in Gwen Poisson, who's probably the second best freelancer this side of the pole. Good morning greetings were exchanged with Gwen.

David sat on the chesterfield and Gwen took the oversized oxblood wingback.

Tina folded her hands in front of her on the desk. "The other night, the Reverend Gary Barlow was murdered in his home."

David nodded. He must have spotted the news on his news service. Gwen just listened.

"He was killed in a rather horrible manner. Someone performed seppuku on him."

Gwen's face had a puzzled expression on it.

"Hara-kiri," David put in and she nodded.

"He was our client. Now, his wife is close to being accused of murder. Her attorney, Harold Feingold, has hired me to get her off the hook. Primarily by finding the killer. Although he'll settle for an alibi which will do the same."

David interrupted. "She doesn't have an alibi?"

"She does. I've spoken with her. She won't use it."

"That seems crazy," Gwen said.

"Agreed. But the choice is ultimately hers."

"What do you want us to do?" David asked.

Tina turned a hand over in David's direction. "Your instructions are simple, David. I want you to find out everything you can on the late Reverend Gary Barlow. Harry will give you what we have."

David nodded.

She turned a hand over in Gwen's direction. "Gwen, I want you to find out everything there is to find out on the Barlow children: Robert and Emily."

"By everything—"

"I mean everything. From the moment they were conceived to the present. I want a complete biography. To be honest, you two, I don't know what I'm looking for. What we know is this: someone killed Barlow. I'm assuming the murder was premeditated due to the manner in which he was sent to the great beyond. I want to know who did it and why. My gut tells me something happened in Barlow's past, or that of his wife, or that of their children to spark his murder. It's remotely possible something happened in the pasts of his parents or his wife's parents. We'll deal with that later, if we have to."

Gwen asked, "Who's checking into Mrs. Barlow?"

"Harry," Tina answered. "He and Bea may be going into business with her, so he should check out what he's possibly getting himself into."

I rolled my eyes. David and Gwen looked at each other and then transferred their looks to me. I filled them in on Celeste Barlow and her new career. That met with no end of chuckles on their parts.

When the hilarity settled down, David asked, "So what's her alibi?"

Tina answered, "She claims she was with the Secretary of State and his wife at the time her husband was killed."

David had a frown on his face. "Seems odd she'd be willing to go down for murder to protect those two. Do you think she's lying?"

"I do and that's what Harry will find out. Anything you two need?"

They indicated they'd wait to see what I sent them and I told them I'd do so right away. They stood, said thanks to Tina, goodbye to both of us, and left.

"So now we want a killer and will settle for an alibi," I said.

"Feingold wants us to find the killer and I think he'll settle for us getting her off the hook, which we can do by providing an alibi. And at this point, Harry, the more I think about it, the more I think run with finding an alibi if you can. As I said yesterday, we'll stick to that angle for now. If she can't be more forthcoming, I really would rather just be done with the case. Besides, I don't want to step on any police toes. Once they charge Celeste, then we will be free to look for the murderer because then we'll be showing she is innocent. Providing we find the murderer."

"You don't want to avenge Barlow? After all, he was our client."

"Vengeance is mine, saith the Lord. Besides the police are on it and they have more manpower than we do. I'm curious, but not that curious. And the sooner we're done with this, the sooner Cal can come over."

"Okay, Boss. And what if she's lying?"

"About who she was with?"

"Yes."

"That is possible. I think the point is she doesn't think whoever she was with will want to alibi her or she doesn't want them involved."

"So the alibi angle may end up being a bust."

"Yes, it may. Which means we'll have to find the murderer."

I as a bit at sea. "If the Rhinelanders aren't the ones who Celeste was with, who was she with?"

"That's your job to find out and if the person will alibi her, then we are done."

I persisted. "What I mean is, if she wasn't with a client who was she with?"

"That's your job to find out."

"What about a little help here?"

"Harry, I'm not clairvoyant. How the hell do I know until you give me some information. So quit gabbing and earn your goddamn paycheck."

She buried her nose in her computer screen and since I wasn't getting anything out of her, I did the same.

I spent the remainder of the morning digging into everything I could find on the internet connected with Celeste Lorraine Barlow, née Collins. She was born in Pennsylvania in 1968. She has an older brother and a younger sister. When she was two, her father sold his company in Pennsylvania, moved the family to Minnesota, and founded a computer company named Computron.

In the '80s, Celeste's father sold Computron for seven hundred million dollars. He gave each of the children five million. By the time the senior Collins died two years ago, bad investments had reduced the Collins wealth to around one hundred million. Celeste's mother is worth somewhat more than that today. Apparently, she has a better financial advisor.

When she was twelve years old, Celeste was shipped off to Groton-Peabody Academy for her junior high and senior high years. Her brother, Bridger, was already there, being three years older. Then three years later Nicole joined Celeste. Bridger, however, was in college by that time. I wondered if those were lonely years or welcome years away from home?

After lunch, which was Mac and Swiss Cheese with bacon crumbles, I decided to get some balmy Minnesota air. And balmy it was with clear skies and a windchill of five below. I drove over to the Barlow residence. The police tape was no longer present to indicate a crime scene. I parked on the street, walked up to the house, and rang the doorbell. I didn't have to wait long for Celeste to answer. Even without makeup and dressed in a sweater and jeans, she'd still look good on a man's arm and make him look good in the process.

"Good afternoon, Celeste."

"Harry Wright. Come in. I just got back from the airport. Picked up the kids."

I crossed the threshold and Celeste closed the door.

"The children are upstairs in their rooms."

"How are they holding up?"

"As well as can be expected, I suppose."

"And yourself?"

"I'll live. I'm not sure the reality of it all has hit me yet."

"Probably not. I'd like to ask a question, if I may?"

"Go ahead."

"What did you and your husband fight about in the driveway when you threatened to kill him?"

She sighed. "Come. Let's sit in the living room."

As with the rest of the house, the living room appeared to have been professionally decorated. Unlike some of the other rooms, it had mostly remained so.

"What do you want to know?" she asked.

"Tell me about it."

"We had been to a party held by an organization where I serve on the board."

"What's the organization?"

"The Lillian Hilger Foundation."

"Never heard of it."

"I'm not surprised. They are a small organization that helps unwed mothers."

"I see. So you and your husband were at a party."

"Yes. I'd had too much to drink and he was giving me crap

about it. Conduct unbecoming of a minister. I told him to go to hell. It was all a sham."

"*It* being…?"

"The church. Religion."

I nodded. "There are reports you threatened to kill him.

"Yes. He kept badgering me all the way home. We pulled into the driveway, I told him to 'fuck off', and got out of the car. He followed, said something, and that was it. I started screaming at him. I think I said something like, 'If you don't shut that piehole, I'm going to shut if for you and you won't be breathing after-wards.' I might have said other things. I don't remember. Rather embarrassing all that. Me screaming in the front yard and the police showing up."

"Who called them?"

"One of the neighbors is my guess."

"What happened when they showed up?"

"Gary gave them some explanation, while I was telling them to fuck off and leave us alone." I smiled at that. Must've been a sight to see. "Eventually they left. After that, we didn't talk about religion or the ministry anymore. Just better for our relationship."

"You know this would be much easier if you simply admitted where you were and who you were with."

"I don't want my children to know."

"And Mr. and Mrs. Rhinelander."

"Yes. I don't want their secret pleasures to be made fun of and to ruin his career."

"Why protect them?"

"I can't say."

"Just so you know, we aren't buying your story."

"Oh?"

"No. Just doesn't ring true. We've seen a lot of cases. They'd have to have a mighty big hold on you and it doesn't seem likely."

She shrugged. "That's my story and I'm sticking to it."

"Suit yourself. Oh, one other question."

"Okay."

"You ask for a lot of personal information on your website."

"You've been on it?"

"Yes."

She smiled. "You will get your money's worth. If you sign up, I'll guarantee you are vetted."

"I have a wonderful wife who satisfies my needs and then some."

"Too bad. But think about it."

"I'll talk it over with Bea. Anyway, you ask for a lot of info. Where does it go?"

"We hold it after the person's been vetted. Off the website server, in case it gets hacked."

"What do you do with it?"

"Just records. If the person passes, they become a member and choose their membership package."

"Is it possible someone got access to the info and for some reason decided to kill your husband?"

"I don't think that is possible. The information isn't online. Only my people and I have access."

I filed it away. The look on her face told me she wasn't trying to hide something, like selling the info to con artists. Or even using it to con.

"May I ask who your people are?"

"You may ask, but I'm not saying. I need to protect their identities."

"Thank you for your time. Tina and I will do our best to get to the bottom of this."

"Thank you. I know you will."

"I'll be on my way."

I stood and Celeste did as well. We walked to the front door and she opened it.

"Harry?"

"Yes?"

"Your wife is very cute. She could make a lot of money. Both of you could. Husband and wife team. MILFs are popular you know. And people like to see a husband and wife. For our videos."

"Thanks, Celeste. I don't think she's interested. She's not money motivated, either. When Bea's spouse died, she inherited a lot of money. Gave away almost a billion dollars. Kept a little for herself, but doesn't touch it."

Celeste let out a little laugh. "Now I know why she looked familiar. She was married to Alicia Harris."

"Yes, she was."

"Well if not for money, the sex is fun. And everybody loves lesbians. A MILF lesbian scenario. I like it."

I chuckled. "I don't like sharing and I don't think Bea does either. And I don't think either of us are keen on people watching."

"Too bad. Do keep it in mind, though, if you ever have a change of heart."

"Bye Celeste."

"Bye Harry."

She leaned in and gave me a peck on the cheek.

I left, got in my car, and sat a moment. Muttering to myself, "Something very odd about his, Harry, ol' boy. Very odd indeed."

I started the car and drove down the block, turned the corner, and parked. I got out and walked back to talk with the neighbors. Perhaps they could clear up some of the mystery. I wasn't overly hopeful, but one never knows.

The snow had stopped falling. There was no wind, which meant the fourteen degrees above zero actually felt like it. Not a heat wave, but, hey, this is Minnesota and we'll take anything we can get above zero.

I started with one of the next door neighbors. They hadn't lived in the house two years ago and hadn't noticed anything unusual the night of the murder. I moved on down the street. When I got to "Reverend Who?", I crossed the street and started working the other side.

The neighbor directly across the street was the one who'd called the police two years ago.

"At two-oh-seven," she said. "Screaming her head off she was going to kill him. She was hitting him and he was trying to hold her arms. Quite a scene it was. Woke me from a dead sleep."

I asked about the night of the murder. She confirmed the open door and that two people entered. Those two, it turned out, were Tina and I. Otherwise, she saw nothing unusual. I thanked her, continued on down the street, and crossed to the other side when people started telling me they had no idea who I was asking about.

The neighbor next door on the other side from where I had started said he remembered Mrs. Barlow screaming "I'll kill you!" at the top of her lungs.

I asked what time and he couldn't remember exactly. Sometime after one-thirty in the morning, he thought. The night of the murder he hadn't seen anything unusual.

Certainly the neighbors's versions of the incident were more colorful than Celeste's. Of course, she'd want to minimize the color and they'd want to maximize it. The truth was probably somewhere in between and, the county attorney to the contrary, probably not all that important. A drunken row.

I was convinced Celeste didn't do the deed, nor did she hire someone. What she was doing was protecting somebody who meant something to her. Of that I was certain and I didn't think Rhinelander and his wife were all that important. Just a smoke screen.

If I had to make a guess, it was somebody in the organization. And now that I knew there was an organization, I began thinking who those persons might be. Friends? Relatives? Acquaintances? And more importantly, how would I find out if Celeste continued to refuse to supply the information?

I walked back to my car and started it. The results of my canvas? Yes, there was an argument on the front lawn and, yes, she had threatened to kill Gary Barlow. The night of the murder, unfortunately, no one saw anything untoward. One for two.

A glance at the clock told me I probably had enough time to call on Celeste's mother. I put the car in gear and took off for Wayzata.

Mom Collins, aka Betty Ann Collins, née Herman, is seventy-one. She'll turn seventy-two later this year. Her primary residence is still the palatial home her husband purchased when the family relocated to Minnesota. Annual gross income from investments is somewhere between two and a half and three point eight million. She maintains a staff of a butler, cook, and housekeeper, who are full-time employees, and a part-time gardener and maintenance man.

I pulled into the long driveway and admired the appearance of seclusion the trees and space gave the place. The Collins home was my idea of where a mansion should be located, not in the city on West Franklin. I parked, walked to the door, and rang the doorbell.

Imagine my supreme surprise when Genevieve, Alicia Harris's butlerette, answered the door. I know Bea gave her a pile of money when she sold the house and no longer needed her services. And knowing Genevieve, she probably socked it away for retirement. Getting a gig with Mrs. Collins was probably a good deal for her. I see now why the Collins's investments were generating more income. Genevieve is a superb manager.

"Well, well, well, Genevieve, long time no see. How are you?"

True to her training, she acted as if I'd been there just yesterday. "I am well, Mr. Wright, thank you. Are you here to see Mrs. Collins?"

"I am. Terrible business about her son-in-law."

"Indeed. Am I wrong in assuming you do not have an appointment?"

"No. Decided to stop by while I was out and about."

"I'll see if she is receiving this afternoon. Please step into the foyer."

"Thank you, Genevieve."

I entered and waited, hat in hand, until Genevieve returned.

"Mrs. Collins will see you," the butlerette announced. She took my hat and coat and led me to a smallish room. I sat and in a few moments a well-dressed woman with dark brown hair entered. I stood and she extended her hand, which I took, and we shook hands.

"I'm Betty Collins."

"Pleased to meet you. I'm Harry Wright." I extracted a business card, gave it to her, and showed her my license.

"You're a private investigator."

"That's correct."

"What are you investigating?"

"Your son-in-law's murder in general and specifically if your daughter, Celeste, was involved. My condolences, by the way."

"Thank you. Most unfortunate. He was a very nice man."

"Death is almost always unfortunate."

"Yes." She sat and indicated I should do the same. "Who hired you?"

"Celeste's attorney."

"I see. The investigation isn't going well for her?"

"She isn't cooperating."

"Sounds like Celeste."

"In what way?"

"She's always been secretive about her affairs and very independent. Even as a child. Ask her what she was doing and she'd say, 'Nothing.' Even when you could see what she was doing and called her on it, she'd say, 'No, I'm not. Just looks that way.'"

"Interesting," I said. "I guess we all have our quirks."

"Indeed we do, Mr. Wright. I can give you an hour. What is it you want to know?"

"Everything you can tell me about Celeste. From her birth to now."

"Probably take me more than an hour, but I'll give you what I can."

And give me a full hour's worth of information she did. If any of it will be useful remains to be seen.

She told me about Celeste's school years and her dating life, her marriage to Gary, her interest in social causes, her proclivity to be quiet and reserved.

In all, I got a lot of surface data and none of it told me the inner working of Celeste Collins. It was as though her mother didn't really know her own daughter. I got the feeling Mrs. Collins didn't and doesn't like Celeste. Views her as a failure: not a good enough student, not a good enough wife, not a good enough mother, not a good enough person.

I have the recording and I have my notes. I'll review them and see if they give me anything I may have missed listening to Mrs. Collins. She advised me to make an appointment through Genevieve, if I needed anything further.

Mentioning Genevieve's name, Mrs. Collins's face positively glowed. "She's a wonderful administrator. In her first six months on the job, she increased my investment yield by three-quarters of a percent. More than enough to pay her salary and benefits."

I smiled. I already knew how good Genevieve was. Had Alicia Harris lived, taken control of Harris Industries, and put Genevieve in charge — I'd have purchased lots of stock, if it was available.

We stood, shook hands, and walked out to the foyer. Genevieve appeared, as if by magic, with my hat and coat. Mrs. Collins and I said, goodbye, and she left.

At the door, I told Genevieve it was good to see her again and wished her her well. She merely said, "Thank you, sir."

The drive home on I-394 was a bear. The worst freeway in the city, if you ask me. Into the CD player I put a disc of Tina playing "Clair de Lune" and other gems and just went with the flow.

9

SUITE FOR ONE

Saturday Night, 8 February

ONCE AGAIN BEA RAIDED MY RECIPE FILE AND MADE *RATATOLHA NIÇA*, an Occitan dish the French call *ratatouille niçoise*, and served it with pasta. She picked out a very nice California Zinfandel to go with the dinner. Couldn't have done better myself. Our conversation revolved around Kazuo Ishiguro's novel *Never Let Me Go* and the ethics of cloning humans. I don't think we solved the problem.

To my mind, it is unsolvable from an ethical standpoint. Because we can't prove if we have a soul or even what is a soul. The question actually is, What makes us human? We have over the millennia come up with all manner of religious and mystical reasons to explain why we are superior to the rest of creation, but in truth are we? Maybe we are just a part of creation and are not better than that which gave us birth. Certainly our actions show we are at times stupider than an amoeba.

Tina summed it well, I think: "If Jesus never wept because he never existed, than what does it matter? Predators all over the planet kill and eat even their own kind. Why do we think we are better when we very much delight in killing each other? And at one time even ate each other and might do so again? With all that why do *we* even bother to weep."

Difficult to argue with her reasoning because in actuality that is how we are, even though we don't like to think so. We don't want to clone ourselves because of the ethics, yet we are very willing to kill ourselves in disregard of those very same ethics. Smacks of hypocrisy if you ask me.

After supper, I went to the office and listened to the recording of my conversation with Celeste's mother and reviewed my notes while I listened. When the recording came to an end, I got ready to listen again.

Tina walked in. "Bea said you were working."

"Listening to my conversation with Celeste's mother."

Tina went to her desk. "Going to play it again?"

"Yep. Just don't call me Sam."

She rolled her eyes. "I'll listen too."

Bea poked her head in. "Hey, guys! It's Saturday night and you're having party without me. I'm crushed."

"Come on in," Tina said.

"Thanks!" Bea went to the chesterfield, tatting in hand, and sat with her feet tucked up under her.

Tina lit a cigar and poured a glass of madeira. I hit "play" and we listened to the interview. When it was over, Tina leaned back in her chair.

"Kind of a messed up family, don't you think?" Bea said.

Tina leaned forward. "Certainly interesting. So Celeste is close with her sister, according to Mom, and not with her brother. In fact, she sees him as little as possible."

"What's more," I put in, "Mom is very disapproving of Celeste in general and especially of her attitude towards her brother."

Bea said, "I get the impression the boy is the favorite."

Tina blew out a cloud of smoke. "Good observation, Bea. I'd even go so far as to wager the favoritism substantially influenced the dynamic among the siblings. That's a valuable piece of information, Harry. Gives us a picture into the family, Celeste, and perhaps why she isn't forthcoming."

"It is. I'll talk to Celeste and her brother and get their views. See if they differ from Mom's."

"Add the sister. I want the entire sibling dynamic from their points of view."

"Okay. All the siblings."

"In fact, see if you can get them to come here. I'd like to talk to them."

"Sure thing, Boss."

"What did you find out from Celeste and her neighbors?"

"I got her version of the late night front yard incident and versions from two of her neighbors. Bottom line? It happened. She admits and the neighbors confirmed she did threaten to kill her husband. Celeste presents a milder version and the neighbors a more colorful one. Basically, she was drunk and Gary didn't like it. According to Celeste, he kept needling her and she finally exploded." I then related what Celeste told me she had said.

"Did anyone see anything the night of the murder?" Tina asked.

"No. Blank slate there."

She nodded.

Bea put her tatting down. "If we could get her cell phone, couldn't we see who she was calling?"

"Yes, we could," Tina replied, "except Sunny Day doesn't use a phone."

Bea looked puzzled. "Who's Sunny Day?"

I clarified. "Sunny Day is Celeste Barlow's alter ego. Sunny Day runs a bordello empire, it seems."

"Really? I didn't even know there was such a thing. And she's really a hooker?"

"Yes, she is."

Tina added, "And your dear husband has been trying to get you a job with Sunny Day and friends."

"What? Harry! How could you? I'm yours."

"It was a joke, Babe. Besides, you're looking smokin' hot these days and—"

"I'm not a hooker or a porn star."

"It was a joke." I shot a look at Tina meant to kill, only she was doing all she could to not burst out laughing. Siblings. Bah!

"I don't like you joking about me having sex with other people."

"Well she said we could do a husband-wife thing—"

"Harry! I'm not making love to you on camera."

Bea was pissed.

Tina intervened. "Sorry I mentioned it, Bea. As Harry said, it was a joke. You had to be there. I'm sorry. But Harry has a point. You are looking very nice these days."

"Thanks. But I don't want to have sex with anyone other than Harry."

"No one is making you, Babe. As I said, it was a joke."

"Okay. If Celeste or Sunny Day or whoever she is doesn't have a phone, how does she run her business?"

I answered, "Email or the contact form on her website,"

Bea's eyebrows went up. "She has a website?"

"Yep. Very high tech.

"I still don't get why she wouldn't use a phone."

"I suppose she's trying to avoid spying," Tina said.

"Oh, sure, I read about that."

Tina continued, "Every government agency in the United States is spying on us. From the federal government down to your local police department. Smart phones in particular make their job much easier because a smart phone is a mini-computer. In under two minutes, a Universal Forensic Extraction Device can steal everything from your phone — even password protected items. Nothing is safe."

Bea's eyes were wide open. "Wow. You get stopped for rolling through a stop sign and the police have your whole life."

"Exactly." Tina was smiling. She likes Bea, but more and more she appreciates these sudden insights Bea gets.

"And our business woman wouldn't want to risk that," I added.

Bea was nodding her head. "I see that. But can't her computer or tablet be hacked?"

"It can," Tina replied. "The process is more difficult and therefore using a computer or tablet and email would give our client a modest amount of security over a smart phone."

Bea was thoughtful. "So where does that leave us?"

Tina answered. "We keep digging until we find what we need to get her off the hook."

I stood. "As in, let's go down to The Hotel Minneapolis, Babe, and find out if they have records for a customer named 'Sunny Day'."

"Oh, boy! I'll drive!" Bea squealed.

I barely suppressed a chuckle. Bea is forty-eight and sometimes she seems like she's sixteen. Maybe that's why Tina's young renter, Solstice Sonata Parker gets along with her so well. They both, at times, seem to be barely out of high school.

————

Twenty minutes later we were talking to the night manager of the hotel.

"Mr. Wright, Ms. Day is a valued customer. I just can't give you that information."

"Mr. Aase, I appreciate your desire to protect your patrons. However, you are aware I could come back with a court order and make you cough up *all* your records. I'm only asking, off the record, for one night and one room."

"I'm sorry, Mr. Wright, I just don't—"

I interrupted him by laying pictures of the Franklin triplets on his desk.

"Just between you and me. Me including my very discreet wife."

He looked at the triplets and licked his lips. "Mr. Wright... I—"

I picked up the pictures of Ben and his brothers. "You are aware, Mr. Aase, prostitution is a crime. I can't imagine what might happen if your boss found out prostitution was going on in this hotel and on your shift. That you were aiding and abetting a criminal. In addition, my friends at the Society for the Rehabilitation of American Sex Workers are looking for a way to put their cause in the public eye. A demonstration in front of the hotel coupled with a news story would be wonderful publicity for them. Don't you think?"

"You're blackmailing me."

"I have a witness who says we were shooting the breeze about this never ending winter."

He tapped keys on his computer. "I have to check on something. If you'll excuse me."

He left and I occupied his chair. I took out my flash drive and downloaded the reservations for the day in question. Then in a fit of generosity, I put one picture of Ben on Aase's keyboard.

"Come on, Bea, we're done."

We left the hotel, walked to where Bea had parked her car, got in, and began the trip home.

On the way back, I could tell she was upset. "Harry?"

"Yes, Bea?"

"You're a very bad man."

"I am?"

"Yes. First you try to turn me into a sex worker and then you threatened that man."

I could see I wasn't going to live down that comment I'd made very easily. Hopefully, I'd have better luck trying to exonerate my behavior with Aase. "I only resorted to threats after he wouldn't take my bribe."

"And that's just as bad. Trying to bribe him."

"Bea, most of the time, heck ninety-eight percent of the time, we're honest to the bone."

She glanced over at me.

"Really. Once in a while, though, we have to lie to get the info we want. Like I did about my friends at the Society for the Rehabilitation of American Sex Workers."

"You did?"

"Yeah. Because I made the group up while we were sitting there."

"Oh, Harry." She let out a giggle. "But you did threaten him with reporting him to his boss and with a court order. That's not right."

"I don't know about that. I'm always Wright."

"Harry."

"Sorry. Tell me this, Bea. When a person calls up and agrees to pay me three hundred dollars to look up something he or she could have looked up for free, am I being dishonest in taking his or her money?"

She started to speak and then stopped.

"Next time, I suppose you'll want me to tell the person where to look and how to get the info for free."

"Well, no, not exactly…"

"Sin of omission or sin of commission. A sin is a sin. Life is full of little sins, my love."

"I know, sweets, but what you did just didn't seem right."

"What if the info gets our client off the hook? What if it stops the only parent those two kids have from going to jail for life?"

"Okay. I see your point."

"Life isn't black and white. Just shades of gray."

She giggled. "Maybe even fifty of them."

"Yeah. Maybe."

Bea pulled into the driveway and parked where it wasn't supposed to be was Solstice's Land Rover. Solstice Sonata Parker is a wannabe artist and just can't seem to understand her garage is the one under her apartment, the former servant's quarters when the place really was a bonafide mansion, and is accessed from the other driveway.

"I'm going to—"

"I will." Bea took out her cell and told it to call "Solstice". She put the phone on speaker.

On the third ring, we heard a Georgia drawl. "Hey, Bebe, how's it hangin'?"

"I don't have anything to hang."

Giggling came from the phone.

"I am doing just fine, though."

"That's awesome, Bebe. What's up?"

"Would you be able to move your car?"

"Oh, shit. I left it out, didn't I?"

"Yep."

"I'll be right down."

"Thanks, Solstice."

"Ciao, Bebe."

Solstice disconnected and in a moment came running out in short shorts that barely covered anything and a skimpy tank top.

I shook my head. "That girl's going to get pneumonia."

Solstice backed her behemoth out to the street and into her driveway and garage, allowing Bea to get her toy car parked. We ran to the house. God, it was cold.

Tina was in the living room, sitting by the fireplace. A cozy wood fire was burning. I just love the smell of a wood fire. Can't stand those gas fireplaces.

"Got anything?" she asked.

"Don't know," I said. "I'm going to look at the data now."

We all went to the office. I plugged the flash drive into my computer and scrolled through the reservations until I found "Sunny Day". She'd booked a suite for one.

10

THE COOL, GREY CITY OF LOVE

Sunday Morning, 9 February

TODAY WAS DAY THREE OF OUR INVESTIGATION AND TO MY MIND, WE were about two inches off of square one. We were certain of one thing: Barlow was dead. We were fairly certain his wife didn't kill him. Other than that, we had not a clue.

For breakfast, I made tea and oatmeal. I was in the mood for something mildly sugary and would stave off the cold. Bea came down just as I was finishing setting the table and was about to partake.

She gave me a kiss. "Good morning, Honey."

"Hi, Babe. Oatmeal's ready."

She sat down, put oatmeal into her bowl, along with milk and brown sugar. Hazelnuts, raisins, and molasses adorned mine.

We were reading the paper, when Tina graced us with her presence. She grunted what I took to be a "good morning". We actually said "good morning" to her.

She looked at my half-eaten bowl of oatmeal and wrinkled her nose. "Oatmeal?"

I confirmed we were indeed eating oatmeal.

She shook her head, sat, and buried her previously wrinkled

nose in her iPad. I poured her a cup of tea. She mumbled something. I took a guess it was a "thank you" and replied, "You're welcome." Just in case. She nodded.

After a couple minutes, Tina looked up and asked, "Bea, is your credit card number 8774-0203-4747-9034, with the security code 763?"

"Geez, I don't know. Why?"

Tina's face was disapproving. "I think one hundred twenty-five dollars for that Victoria's Secret babydoll outfit is a bit much."

Bea's eyes were like the full moon on a cloudless night.

I said, "Babe, you've just been hacked."

"But, I mean... Oh, shit. Really?"

Tina burst out laughing. "Everything on your phone is now right here." She tapped the iPad.

"B-but how?"

"Gwen jailbroke my iPad, added a UFED app of her own making, and now I can do what the police do."

"Oh, wow. Uh, you aren't going to keep my information. Are you?"

"No, Bea. I'm not. But now you know why Celeste doesn't want to run her business using a smart phone."

"Yeah."

"Uh, Babe, when do I get to see you in your new outfit?"

Bea giggled. "It was going to be a surprise, but, now that you know, soon. Real soon."

"I can't wait."

We finished our breakfast and Bea and I started in on the cleanup. Tina stood, announced she'd be in the music room, and departed.

To Bea, I said, "Huh. Looks like she isn't working on the Sabbath."

The strains of Warlock's "Pavane", from the *Capriol Suite*, emanated from the music room.

"Wonder who died?"

Bea hit my arm. "Harry. Be nice. She's your sister."

"I am nice."

Bea gave me a look which was interrupted by a knock on the back door. I went to see who it was. Solstice was standing outside in the absolutely freezing weather. I knew it was freezing because Buddy hadn't wanted to stay out for very long not more than a couple hours ago. But looking at Solstice, one would think it was summer. She had on a very short skirt and a long sleeve blouse with half the buttons unbuttoned. Pneumonia. She was asking for it. I opened the door and invited her in.

"Hi, Harry! Is Bebe around?"

Bea joined me.

"There you are!" Solstice gave Bea a big hug. "You want to go shopping, Bebe?"

Bea looked at me.

Solstice said, "I can loan you money, if you need it."

"I'm good," Bea told her.

I nodded my head in the direction of the music room. "Fine with me, Hon. Tina's at a funeral and I have work to do."

Bea rolled her eyes and Solstice got all solemn. "Oh. Who died?"

"He's just trying to be funny. Ignore him. Sure. I'd love to go shopping."

"Great! Let's leave in an hour. I'm driving."

"Okay, Solstice."

"I'll give ya a call, when I'm leaving. Laters! Bye, Harry."

Solstice always makes her farewell to me sound like the conclusion of a wet dream with the promise of more. In a normal tone of voice, I replied,"Bye, Solstice," and closed the door behind her.

"You really don't mind me going shopping?"

"Mind? Why would I mind? Have fun. Solstice will even lend you money if you run out."

"One of these days I should probably tell her."

"Why? I think it hilarious the little rich kid thinks you're poor."

"It kind of is. What are you going to do today?"

"Keep working the case. Should probably find out from the Boss if she wants Ed to work on some aspect of it or not."

From Warlock's "Pavane", Tina had moved to "Sung to Sleep", and from there to *Pavane for a Dead Princess*.

"Drat," I said. "Should've caught her on 'Sung to Sleep'. Oh, well."

"I'm going upstairs to change, Harry."

"Okay, Babe. I'll be conferring with the Red Baron."

Bea hit my arm and went on upstairs, while I made my way to the music room. I waited until the final note of the "Pavane" had been played to ask, "Do you want Ed to work on something? I should let him know."

Tina sighed. "Let's go to the office."

She doesn't like to discuss work outside the office. Doesn't want it intruding into the rest of her life. Probably why the office is the smallest part of the house. We walked to the Inner Sanctum of Wright Investigations.

I saw Tina look at Bea's empty desk. "Where's Bea?"

"She and Solstice are going shopping."

"Funny how Solstice has taken to her. Kind of adopted her, even though Bea is almost twice her age."

"Isn't it, though? Who would have thought? Solstice even offered to loan Bea money, if she needed it."

Tina let out a laugh. "That's rich. If she only knew."

"Right."

We sat at our respective desks. Tina took a cigar from the humidor and lit it, puffed on it, then took a big drag, and blew a cloud of smoke towards the ceiling.

"Have David and Gwen checked in?" I asked.

"Not yet. Talked to Cal while you were out last night. The police are just as stumped as we are. All roads lead to Celeste, for them anyway, even though they can't actually put her at the scene when Barlow was murdered."

"And that's the reason why she hasn't been charged yet?"

"That, coupled with my statement to Cal she has an alibi, seems to have them and the county attorney treading more carefully."

"What do you want Ed to do?"

She sent a cloud of smoke to the ceiling. "I'd like him to check out Celeste's brother. See if he can find anything giving the brother a reason to want Barlow dead — no matter how flimsy."

"Do you still want to talk to the siblings?"

Tina looked at the ceiling, then at me. "Hold off on the siblings. Let's see what Ed comes up with. I'm also switching Gwen's assignment, so have her come in to report and get the new assignment."

Bea came in, kissed me goodbye, and left on her shopping expedition.

"I'd like to talk to David and find out what he knows about the church situation. I'm thinking I need to head over there and I don't want to cover ground he's already walked on."

"Okay. Call them both in."

I got on the phone and was surprised when I saw Tina do the same. My calls didn't take long and when I looked at Tina, she jotted a note and pushed it to the edge of her desk. I got up and retrieved it. There was one word on it: "Hovhaness".

Alan Hovhaness Brown, his musician parents named him after their favorite composer, worked for MI6, retired, moved to the States, married, became a US citizen, and got his PI license in New York City. He and Tina met while working on an espionage case a couple years or so before she left the CIA.

She chatted with Hovhaness for around a half-hour, when their call ended, she turned to me. "I want someone to checkout Groton-Peabody. If there is something of interest on the Barlow kids, it probably happened at school."

"Makes sense."

"Hovhaness gave me the names of two PIs in Massachusetts: Dominic Famiglietti and Elena Urban. Both in Boston. According to Hovhaness they are top drawer."

"You want me to call?"

"No. I'll call."

Always good to see the Boss earn a little bit of the client's money. She called Famiglietti first and discovered he wasn't available. Elena Urban was, however, and agreed to do some digging for us. With that done, Tina lit a fresh cigar and poured herself a glass of madeira. A reward for a hard day's work.

"Did Gary Barlow have siblings?" Huh. She's still on the clock.

"Don't know. Easy enough to find out." Once again my finger got a workout on the desk phone.

On the second ring, she answered.

"Hi, Celeste."

"Hello, Harry. How are you?"

"Fine, thanks. You doing okay?"

"I'm holding it together."

"Good. I have a quick question."

"Okay."

"Gary have siblings?"

"Yes. A younger sister. About ten years younger. Something of a wild thing. Thrice married and thrice divorced. Each divorce due to her infidelity."

"She live here?"

"No. Virginia. I'll email the address."

"Thanks. His parents?"

"They live in Connecticut. I'll email their address, too. By the way, the three of them should be here tomorrow."

"For the funeral?"

"Yes. They'll be staying at my mother's."

"Thanks for the information, Celeste."

"Uh, Harry?"

"Yes?"

"I'll give you a first time customer discount."

"Thanks, but—"

"For you and your wife. Keep it in mind."

"I will. Thanks. Bye."

"Goodbye, Harry."

I hung up the phone and just sat there. Finally Tina gave me a verbal nudge. "Well?"

"Yes. He does. A younger sister who lives in Virginia. His parents live in Connecticut and all three are arriving tomorrow. They'll be staying with Celeste's mom. And Celeste offered me a first time customer discount. When I balked, she included Bea."

"Really?"

"Scout's honor."

"I think she likes you, Harry."

"Not my cup of tea."

The doorbell rang. I got up and answered the door. Gwen was outside and I invited her in.

"Hey, Harry!"

"Hi, Gwen."

She gave me a hug and bussed my cheek.

"Go on in. Want a cucumber water?"

"You're so sweet. Sure."

Gwen went on in to the Inner Sanctum and I went to the kitchen to get her cucumber water. Cool water in a smallish pitcher, thinly sliced Persian cucumbers dropped into the water, and a glass. I put pitcher and glass on a tray and carried it to the office.

The girls were shooting the breeze when I entered. Tina doesn't have many friends. Gwen, though, is one. Tina isn't close to many people either. However when Gwen got kidnapped a couple years back working on a case for us, Tina was worried sick about her. When she was returned by the kidnappers, Tina made her stay with us until the case was over. They highly respect each other.

I set the tray on the little table by the oxblood wingback where Gwen was sitting and poured her a glass of water.

"Thanks, Harry."

"You're welcome, Gwen."

I sat at my desk and the doorbell rang. Out to the front door I went, saw David standing on the other side and let him in.

"Hi, Harry."

We shook hands while I said "Hi" back and then made our way to the Inner Sanctum where David exchanged greetings with the ladies and took a seat on the chesterfield. I asked him if he wanted anything and he said first prize at the next bonsai show, otherwise he was good. I told him I'd see what I could do and he thanked me in advance for my efforts.

"What I'd like first is a report on what you two have discovered," Tina said.

Gwen began. "Nothing out of the ordinary. Those are two normal kids. Good kids. Aren't in any trouble. At least that I could find. I haven't checked out their lives at Groton-Peabody, but here? They're cool."

"Thanks, Gwen. I'm giving you a new assignment. I want you to find out all you can on Celeste's sister, Nicole Anastasia Collins."

"Okay. I'll get on it right away."

"What have you found out, David?"

"I started at the church and worked backwards, although there is plenty to mine at the church."

"How so?" Tina asked.

"Infighting," he replied.

Tina nodded and told him to continue.

"Spoke with one of the secretaries. An older woman, Lois Gorman. The police had already been there."

Tina nodded.

"And she was reluctant to talk to me. Bought her lunch and that broke the ice. Seems Reverend Barlow's future vision for the church was not to the liking of Phebe Vander Walle, who is chairperson of the deacon board, and Nils Brodigan, who's the Council Moderator. They've openly disagreed with Barlow's plan. Made it a major church issue to the point where a push had been started to force Barlow out."

"Tares among the wheat," Tina quipped.

David had a puzzled look on his face. Tina, however, indicated he should continue, which he did.

"Naomi Frame, who was Coordinator for Youth Activities and Community Ministries, and James Vander Walle, who is Church Treasurer and Phebe's husband, were having some kind of dispute. Lois was a bit vague about what. I suppose it doesn't matter. In the end, Naomi accused James of having an affair with Celeste Barlow. James and Celeste denied they were involved in an affair and Naomi was forced to resign. Seems people came to believe Naomi made up the story to get back at James. He had apparently won their dispute.

"And finally, Emily Stevens, the Assistant Minister for Hospitality, and Gary Barlow had been spending a lot of time together for the better part of a year. Rumors were flying about an affair. Both denied they were romantically or sexually involved with each other, but the rumors persisted. Perhaps helped along by Phebe and Nils as part of their campaign to get Gary Barlow to leave."

Gwen said, "Wow. I didn't know church could be so exciting. I might have to start attending."

Tina chuckled. "You need to work in the church to get the juicy stuff."

David continued. "I didn't pursue the church lines of inquiry. I figured if any of them were likely suspects, the police would've been on them like bees to honeysuckle."

"I agree," Tina said. "Anything else, David?"

"Yes. Reverend Barlow had a missing year."

"Celeste mentioned it," Tina said.

David went on. "I traced his movements to Las Vegas and then encountered problems."

"How so?" Tina asked.

"He basically disappears. I had a business associate out there do some digging for me. There are indications he stayed a night or two in Vegas after he flew into town, before leaving. Destination unknown. Can't track him any further."

Tina turned to her computer. After a few minutes she asked us to gather around her desk, which we did.

"Last night I went over the pictures Harry took of the Barlow residence before the police got there." She brought up photos I'd taken of three poems, written in calligraphy, and framed. "I found these of interest." She pointed to one of the poems. "Especially this one."

I read the lines:

> *Tho the dark be cold and blind,*
> *Yet her sea-fog's touch is kind,*
> *And her mightier caress*
> *Is joy and the pain thereof;*
> *And great is thy tenderness,*
> *O cool, grey city of love!*

Tina tapped the screen. "However, I couldn't place them. So I did a search. The poems are by George Sterling. He lived in San Francisco, was championed by Ambrose Bierce, and hailed as the next American Poet Laureate by H. L. Mencken. His fame never materialized and he committed suicide in 1926. Those six lines are the concluding lines of his poem to San Francisco, "The Cool, Grey City of Love", which can be found on a plaque in George Sterling Glade. I saw the plaque when I lived in San Francisco."

David had a big smile on his face. "You think he went to San Francisco."

"Yes."

"I'm on it."

"Oh, and David?"

"Yes?"

"I think there may have been a love interest because of this poem." She pointed to the one she felt indicated Gary had a girl-friend there.

Happiest

Calling you now, not for your flesh I call,
Nor for the mad, long raptures of the night
And passion in its beauty and its might,
When the ecstatic bodies rise and fall.
I cannot feign: God knows I see it all—
The flaming senses, raving with delight,
The leopards, swift and terrible and white,
Within the loins that shudder as they crawl.

All that could I exultingly forego,
Could I but stand, one flash of time, and see
Your heavenly, entrancing face, and know
I stood most blest of all beneath the sun,
Hearing these words from your fond lips to me:
"I love, love you, and love no other one!"

David smiled. "Yeah, I can see that. Okay, Miss Wright, I'm on it."

"Good."

We returned to our seats and Tina said, "As usual you two have been very helpful. Let's see if we can't yet find our killer."

With the party over, I gave each additional expense money and told David to make sure he sent me the bill for the work his business associate did. He assured me he would. I escorted them to the door and bid them farewell. When I saw they were safely on their way, I returned to our own holy of holies.

Tina was still at her desk. Her eyes were closed and she was leaning back in her chair. Most likely lost in thought. I sat and waited, hoping she'd open her eyes and tell me the Gordian Knot had been unravelled. When she did open them, she looked at me and said, "Get Celeste."

That was what I didn't want to hear.

11

"YOU'RE FIRED"

Sunday Night, 9 February

Tina and Celeste were looking at each other. No words were being exchanged. None at present, that is. Previously, the words that had been traded ended up solving nothing.

Celeste had been reluctant, but finally agreed to come to our place. She was sitting in the oxblood oversized wingback. Her attire was a fairly modest pair of slacks and a blouse. Tina was wearing her usual skirt suit. A gray pinstripe, as it happened to be, with pleated skirt.

After greetings were exchanged, Tina began the fruitless exchange with, "Who were you with the night your husband was murdered?"

Celeste responded with, "I've already told you."

To which Tina said, "You're lying."

Celeste merely shrugged.

Tina continued, "You are making this investigation unnecessarily complex."

Celeste said, "I don't have to provide an alibi if I don't want to do so. If you're as good as Harold says you are, you should be able to solve this without knowing who I was with."

Tina was steamed. I could tell by the look on her face. Mostly because Celeste was telling her to work and Tina doesn't want to work if she doesn't have to. In addition to the look on her face, I know she was steamed by what she said next.

"I will hack your website, get the information I need to get you off the hook, and then I will completely wipe it clean."

Now you know why they were no longer talking. When it became apparent this was going to be a marathon stare down, I started timing. Eleven minutes and forty-two seconds passed before Celeste stood.

She said two words. "You're fired."

Tina replied, "You didn't hire me. Feingold did."

To which Celeste said, "Then he's fired. Harry, my coat please."

I retrieved her coat, the floor length fur, and I escorted her to the door. Or maybe she escorted me. At the door, she touched my arm.

"I like you, Harry, and your wife is very cute. I'd like the two of you to work for me. You will make a lot of money. More than you can dream of. Think about it. In the meantime, goodbye."

She kissed my cheek. Her perfume was very subtle, slightly spicy and musky. Her hand wandered down to my butt where it gave my other cheek a squeeze.

I watched her walk down the walk to her car. She got in and drove off. I closed the door and returned to the Inner Sanctum. Tina was at her desk, staring at the oxblood wingback.

"What on earth did you tell her that for?"

"Shut up, Harry."

"She offered Bea and me jobs. I don't know. I'm thinking maybe to take her up on her offer. She said we'd become rich."

"You're already rich. Shut up."

"I mean, I can see where you both can be unreasonable. But, hey, maybe more money makes the unreasonableness easier to bear."

"Shut up."

"I'm going to find Bea. See what she thinks."

I left the office and found Bea in the living room by the fire. She'd been with Solstice most of the day. They even ate supper together. Some upscale Asian restaurant. Now she was enjoying the fire and tatting."

"Hi Harry! Meeting over?"

I kissed her and sat next to her. "Yep. Tina got us fired."

"She did? We're unemployed? I do have that money, you know."

"We don't have to worry."

"We don't?"

"Nope. Sunny Day has offered us jobs in her sex empire. Said we'd become rich."

"We're already rich."

"Yeah, well, I didn't tell her that. Anyway, money is the least of our worries."

"That's a good feeling. Isn't it, Harry?"

"It is."

"Did Mrs. Barlow really fire us?"

"Since she didn't hire us, she can't fire us. So to fire us, she fired her lawyer. Well, that's what she said she was going to do. We'll see if she actually fires him or merely tells him to not use our services. In either case, I think this job is at an end."

"I'm hungry, Harry. That Chinese food never lasts long."

"Wouldn't mind a snack myself. White Castle?"

"Ooh. Yummy. You sure know how to get to a girl's heart."

I couldn't help but laugh. "I know how to get to this girl's heart and that's all that matters."

"Come on, lover boy. I'll drive."

Bea drove us over to my favorite White Castle in Nordeast, where they know me by name. We decided on a dozen sliders, a dozen cheese sliders, a sack of onion chips, a sack of fries, and a couple orange pops. Yeah, I know. I hate pop. The things a person does for love. We sat in the Castle and downed sliders. The nice thing about being in love is you don't have to say a whole lot to the other person. Usually looks say way more than words.

When we were full, we took the uneaten food with us to the car and on to the castle on West Franklin we call home. We came in through the back door, put the leftovers in the fridge. No music was coming from the music room and Tina wasn't in the living room, library, or game room. Nor was she in the kitchen or dining room. We found her in the office, sitting behind her desk, a scowl on her face.

"There are—" I started to say when Tina interrupted.

"She is a pompous and arrogant ass."

Bea and I looked at each other.

"And you two are *not* going to work for her. Do you understand me?"

"Are you going to give us a raise?" I asked.

"Shut up and sit down. Shit. My own brother leaving me to work for some goddamn rich ho."

I sat at my desk and Bea sat on the chesterfield.

"Are you okay working for her, Bea?" I hooked my thumb in Tina's direction.

"Of course she is," Tina said.

Bea said, "Uh, actually I do like it here. I like being with you two. I love you. What's going on?"

I waved my hand, dismissing Tina's tirade. "She's just pissed."

The scowl reappeared and was cast in my direction. "Harry, call Gwen."

"Tina, I'm not calling Gwen. We aren't hacking the Sunny Day site."

"Then I'll call her."

"Go ahead, but why don't we sleep on this? I don't think we should piss off Celeste before we know we're fired for sure."

Bea got up, went to Tina, hugged her, and kissed her cheek. Then sat back down on the chesterfield.

"What was that for?" Tina asked.

"I love you and I don't want you to be angry."

Tina sighed. "Okay. I'll leave it. For now."

"Whew," I said. "Peace in our time."

Tina leaned back in her chair, her fingers steepled. "David's looking into the missing year of Gary Barlow and has uncovered the turmoil at the church. In addition, we now know Celeste and James Vander Walle may have had an affair—"

"Or he was one of her customers," I interrupted.

"Yes. He may have been a client," Tina concurred. She continued, "We also know Emily Stevens and Reverend Gary were close enough for a period of time to spark rumors something more than work was going on. Which means, Emily Stevens is a potential suspect and so is James Vander Walle."

"I think we need to add Phebe Vander Walle and Nils Brodigan to the suspect list," I said.

"Yes, Harry, I agree. Either or both could have decided to get their way by getting Gary Barlow out of the way." Tina sat up. "Get all four of them here as soon as you can."

"Together or separately?"

Tina thought a moment. "Separately, I think will be better."

"Okay, I'll see what I can do. Oh, do you still want to talk to the siblings?"

She thought a moment. "No. Let's see what Ed and Gwen find out first."

"Okay. I'll call the church people."

After another few moments of silence on Tina's part, she said more to herself than to Bea or me. "Seppuku. Why seppuku?"

12

FORGERIES AND DECEPTION

Monday Morning, 10 February

MONDAY BEGAN LIKE ANY OTHER DAY. BUDDY WAS WHINING AT THE back door and I let him out, making sure the chain was securely fastened to prevent him from wandering off. God, it was cold out there. I'm very thankful for indoor plumbing.

I ran through the list of the day's chores while making breakfast. I had those four people to call and I had Celeste herself to continue to investigate. I'd need to make a grocery list for Bea.

Buddy's barking interrupted my thoughts. I went to the door and let him in. No sooner had he shaken the snow off, than Manly pounced on him and the day began in earnest.

Bea joined me in the kitchen and from the music room I heard a Scarlatti sonata. Not a good sign, that. Tina rarely plays baroque keyboard works. Must've got up on the wrong side of the bed this morning. Bea, on the other hand, was her bubbly self and looked stunning in a dark blue knee-length belted shirt dress which added lots of curves to her boyish figure.

"You like it?" she asked.

"That's one of your new acquisitions?"

"Mm-hm." She did a little twirl.

"Looks stunning. Maybe we should quit our jobs here and join Sunny Day's sex empire."

"Oh, Harry. What would we do there?"

"I don't know what I'd do, but you could be a main draw."

"Oh, go on. Who'd pay to have me on his arm?"

"As you look right now? I dunno. Whoever might want Emma Watson on his arm."

"Cut it out, Harry."

"I'm serious, Bea. You're lookin' mighty hot these days. Smokin'."

"Maybe you'd like to take this dress off me and see what else I bought?"

"Mm. Now that sounds like a very good idea."

Tina's voice interrupted. "Tea ready?"

"Tina, you have the worst timing." Bea had a big pout on her face. "Harry was just about to strip me naked and carry me off to bed."

"Sorry," she mumbled. "Don't mind me."

"That's okay, Boss, business before pleasure," I said, "and we have lots of business today."

Bea left her pout on and helped me carry the tea, pastries, fruit, and cheese to the dining room.

There was nothing out of the ordinary about our breakfast routine and, when we'd finished eating, Tina went to the office, while Bea and I cleaned up the dishes and put the food away. That chore finished, she and I took up our respective positions in the office.

Tina was at her desk. Cigar lit and glass of madeira poured. I looked at the clock. The time was eight minutes after nine. The phone rang. Bea answered and in a minute her voice came over the intercom.

"Mr. Feingold's on the phone and he's not very happy."

"Who does he want to speak to?" I asked.

"Tina."

"Put him through," the Great Detective said.

Bea did and Tina put the phone on speaker.

"Good morning, Mr. Feingold," Tina began.

"Don't 'good morning' me, Miss Wright. What the hell is going on? I got an earful from Celeste Barlow. She's fired me, rehired me, fired me, and rehired me. And that is where we're currently at."

"She and I had a difference of opinion yesterday."

"Mrs. Barlow said you threatened her."

"I was trying to persuade her."

"She's not happy you're working on her case."

"Sorry to hear that."

"She'd rather have Harry working on it."

I got up and ran out to our waiting room. I was successful. The laugh burst out with only Bea as audience. When I got the laughter under control, I returned to the office.

Tina was speaking. "As I said, Mr. Feingold, Harry *is* working on Mrs. Barlow's case. I'm not directly involved."

Feingold said, "Very well, then. I'll let her know. Goodbye."

And before Tina could reciprocate, the dial tone had replaced Feingold's voice.

"Where did you go?" she asked.

"The waiting area. I didn't want Feingold hearing me laugh."

Tina nodded. She also had a smirk on her face.

"I guess that means we're still employed," I said.

"I guess it does," she replied. "Now you can call those people."

"Number one on my list."

"Good." She picked up *The Art Forger's Handbook* by Eric Hebborn, sighed, and began reading.

I interrupted, "What was the sigh for?"

She looked at me. "If you must know, envy for the master." She returned her attention to the book.

Envy for the master? Hebborn better than Tina? Huh. He must've been able to fool God, because Tina can fool everyone else.

I got on the phone and began working on appointments for our four suspects. Emily Stevens I got to agree to see Tina at two. Nils Brodigan told me to go hell. Phebe Vander Walle said she had already talked to the police and wasn't interested in any further interrogation. Her husband, James, was evasive. Finally, I insinuated Celeste had said something and Tina wanted to hear from him if two plus two made four. He agreed to see her at five today.

Now I had to come up with some manner of leverage to get Nils and Phebe to see the error of their ways in refusing to talk with the Great Detective.

I called Cal.

"Hey, Major, what's up?"

"I was wondering if you had talked with Nils Brodigan or Phebe Vander Walle?"

"Is this the Barlow case?"

"Oh, sorry. Yes, it is."

"Let me check. I don't think so." There was a pause and then, "No. Wasn't me. It was Nelson who talked to them. Why?"

"Just wondering if you found anything useful or of interest."

"Are you fishing?"

"I like fish."

"Uh-huh. What, the Red Baron wants to talk to them and they don't want to talk to her?"

"You could say that."

He chuckled. "Sorry. Can't help you. But seeing they aren't behind bars ought to tell you something."

"It does. Thanks."

"You're welcome."

I hung up the phone and pondered my next plan of attack. Phebe and Nils were Barlow's antagonists. They probably had decent alibis as well as insufficient motive. So what if I insinuated Tina had gotten hold of information casting doubt on their stories and she wanted to discuss it with them before turning it over to the police. Might work. I bounced the idea off the Boss.

Tina thought for a moment and then gave my ruse the go

ahead. I called Nils back. He said I was a liar, implied I came from a long line of liars, and that he didn't associate with liars. I was left with the dial tone buzzing in my ear. He was one tough nut to crack. I moved on to Phebe, applied sufficient pressure, and she cracked. Phebe thought my suggestion to meet with Tina in her office at eleven tomorrow was a very good idea.

I decided to tackle the recalcitrant Nils Brodigan after lunch and made for the kitchen. California Barley Bowl was on the menu. Cooked barley, arugula, ricotta, nuts, lemon juice, and lemon zest were mixed together. Then I made the yogurt sauce, added sliced avocado, and we were ready. Alexis Bailly Country White was my wine pick. I announced to the ladies luncheon was served.

Tina took one look and said, "Is this another vegetarian dish?"

I confessed it was.

She glowered at me, turned to Bea, and said, "Bea, you're making supper and it better include meat."

Lunch passed in relative silence, a sure sign of Tina's unhappiness, although at one point she did carry on about the importance of lead-tin yellow in the art forger's palette.

Maybe next time I'll put vegan bacon crumbles on top and see if she can spot a forgery.

13

STEVENS AND VANDER WALLE

Monday Afternoon, 10 February

EMILY STEVENS WAS LATE. A WHOLE ELEVEN MINUTES LATE. WHEN Bea showed her in, I escorted her to the oxblood wingback. She was wearing light blue slacks, a white blouse, and a light blue cardigan. One of those oversized ones, with extra long sleeves. I introduced Tina and myself and then sat at my desk. My part completed, the time had come for Tina to shine.

Before Tina began her inquisition, Emily blurted out, "We weren't lovers."

Tina replied, "But you were in love with him."

Even from my desk, I could tell Emily was fighting a meltdown. No words came out. She just nodded her head.

Tina continued the questioning. "He ever kiss you?"

She shook her head. "No. I, I kissed him once and he said we couldn't go down that road. I was hoping he'd want to leave Celeste, but he said that wasn't going to happen either. I didn't kill him, Miss Wright. I loved him."

"Wouldn't be the first time, Reverend Stevens, a jilted lover killed the object of her love."

"But I didn't. I swear I didn't. The police don't believe me either. I was home, alone, while he was…"

That was it. The dam broke and the tears and sobs followed. If it was an act, it was a damn good one. I got up and gave her a box of tissues. At the rate she was going, she'd need it. When she'd gotten her emotions under control, Tina continued.

"If you didn't kill Reverend Barlow, who did?"

"I, I don't know. He was such a nice man. I know there were people who wanted him to leave or change his policies. He wasn't going to do that. He was committed."

"Did you notice anything suspicious in the days and weeks prior to his death?"

"What do you mean?"

"I don't know. You knew him better than I. Was he agitated? Upset? Quiet? Did he have strange visitors? Was there anything different from the normal routine?"

She thought for quite a while. At last she said, "I remember Lois, that's Lois Gorman, one of our secretaries, saying an Asian man had been asking about Reverend Barlow. Gary, though, wasn't in at the time. Lois said the man gave her a business card. She said the card wasn't in English. The letters were Chinese or Japanese."

"What did Ms. Gorman do with the card?" Tina asked.

"She put it on Gary's desk."

"Did Gary have any reaction on seeing the card?"

"Honestly, I don't remember. This was about a month ago. Maybe Lois might know. Gary never mentioned the card to me."

"Did Ms. Gorman tell you this information directly or did you overhear it?"

"I overheard her telling one of the other secretaries."

Tina leaned back in her chair, her chin resting on steepled fingers. Her gaze focused on the Reverend Stevens. For her part, Emily stared mostly at her folded hands. She did favor me for a moment with a quick, nervous glance and smile. I smiled back.

Finally Tina said, "Thank you, Reverend Stevens. I am sorry for your loss."

Emily nodded.

I stood and the Reverend also. I escorted her out to the waiting area, where Bea did the honors of guiding her back out into the cold, cruel world.

Back at my desk, I saw Tina was still focused on the oxblood wingback. Her chin was resting on steepled fingers.

"Let me guess," I said, "you want to talk to Lois Gorman."

"Yes."

"Okay. I'm on it."

I telephoned the church and spoke to Lois. She had never heard of the famous detective Justinia Wright and was not convinced she needed to talk to her. I reminded her of her conversation with David Nagasawa and that David worked for Miss Wright. Lois wavered. I poured on the charm, appealed to her vanity, and also to her grandchildren. She has five. I told her each child would probably love to have a little piece of paper with Ben Franklin's picture on it and all Lois had to do to fulfill their desires would be to come to the office and pickup said pieces of paper. There was a long pause. I was thinking fifty-fifty she was going to hang up on me, when she asked what time. I suggested eight would be wonderful and she concurred. Then we said goodbye.

Before I could say anything, Tina said, "I heard."

"Good," I replied. "I hate repeating myself."

She stood. "I will be in the music room until Vander Walle arrives."

"Cheerio!"

She left and, since I wasn't making supper, I stayed at my desk and thought over my next move in ferreting out everything there was to know about Celeste Barlow, aka Sunny Day.

I called her home phone, but there was no answer. She was probably at her mother's place visiting with Gary's family. I dialed Cal's number.

"Swenson."

"Hey, Cal. Harry, here."

"What's the Red Baron want this time?"

"Nothing. I'm asking on my own."

"Shoot."

"Did you folks take the Barlows's computers and records?"

"We did."

"Leave anything behind?"

"Probably not intentionally."

"That's what I thought. Thanks."

"Why do you want to know?"

"Save myself a trip."

"Oh. Anything else?"

"Would you mind sharing?"

"Yes."

"Thought so. Catch you later."

"See you, Major."

I hung up and pondered how Celeste had emailed me information when the police had their computers. It seemed quite obvious to me they'd overlooked or missed some device. Or maybe it was a device she had hidden. On the other hand, she could have gone to the library or used one of her kids' laptops (what kid doesn't have a laptop these days?). The point is, she has access most likely to someone's computer. One the police don't have. I wonder if maybe this computer the police don't have is the one she conducts her business on. Food for thought, there.

Bea stuck her head in and blew me a kiss. "I'm off to make supper!"

I blew her a kiss back. "Okay, Babe."

She disappeared leaving me to take care of the door and the phone.

After a few moments, I phoned the Collins residence. Genevieve answered.

"Hi, Genevieve! Harry Wright, here."

"Good afternoon, Mr. Wright. The family is not receiving at present."

"Quite all right. I actually just need to ask you."

"Go ahead."

"Is Celeste Barlow there?"

"Not at present."

"Her children?"

"They are here."

"Great. Thanks a million. A good day to you, Genevieve."

"And to you, sir."

I hung up the phone. Hm. No answer at the house and not at her mother's. Where, oh where, has little Celeste gone? Where, oh where, can she be? A look at the clock told me I'd have to put Celeste on the shelf for the time being and prepare for James Vander Walle's arrival.

Snacks and something to drink is always recommended, so I made a trip to the kitchen to secure a selection of canapés and a variety of beverage choices. The goods were placed on a cart and wheeled to the office. Back to the kitchen to secure tea for myself and then to my desk to await our guest's arrival.

Tina walked in a few minutes before five and sat at her desk. A moment later the doorbell rang and I got up to answer the door.

On our doorstep was a tallish man, somewhere in his fifties. He wore no hat to muss his carefully coiffed hair, but did have ear caps on to protect against the elements. His overcoat, even to my eyes, was of very fine quality and a deep, dark, rich brown. I opened the door.

"I'm James Vander Walle. I have an appointment with Ms. Wright." His voice was a pleasing tenor.

"*Miss* Wright is expecting you. I'm her brother and assistant, Harry."

I offered him my hand and by his reaction I could tell he wasn't used to shaking hands with the staff. But he did shake mine. I suppose he didn't want to appear rude, even though he radiated rudeness, and maybe because I was the Great Detective's brother he made an exception. Who knows?

He entered and in the waiting area I took his coat, which revealed the exquisite suit he was wearing. A very nice charcoal number that positively reeked of money.

"Very nice suit," I said.

"Thank you," he replied and when I didn't ask, volunteered, "It's a Brioni Vanquish II."

I smiled, "As I said, a nice suit."

He gave me a brief smile of toleration and then I led him into the Inner Sanctum.

Tina was standing. I made introductions and led him to the oxblood wingback, where he remained standing until Tina sat. When she did, she gestured to the cart.

"Help yourself to some refreshments, Mr. Vander Walle."

"Thank you," he replied.

He looked over the selection of beverages, chose the Beefeater 24, added ice to a glass, and poured in a couple fingers of gin. He nosed his drink, took a sip, and said, "Nice." His attention then focused on Tina.

The two eyed each other for a few moments. Boxers sizing up the opponent, seeing who would give in and pronounce the first word. Tina's very good at this game. She's had practice. Years of practice. The mental dance didn't last overly long. Perhaps Mr. VW was in a hurry.

He said, "The rumors are unfounded. Regardless of what anyone says."

"What rumors are those, Mr. Vander Walle?"

"Are we going to play games, Miss Wright?"

Ah, he was listening. In spite of my staff status.

Tina answered, "No. No games. However, there are many rumors. To which ones are you referring?"

"Many rumors? To which are *you* referring?"

"The SEC investigation, for example."

I have to say he was good. The falter was very slight. I almost missed it.

"Many rumors, indeed. Very well, then, Miss Wright, since your assistant mentioned Mrs. Barlow I made the assumption you wanted to talk about those rumors. And *those* rumors are unfounded. Very definitely so." He took a sip of gin.

"Why should I believe you, instead of Mrs. Barlow?"

He took another sip of gin, paused a moment to give himself an air of reflection or thought, and said, "Mrs. Barlow is a troubled woman. A veritable lost soul. Ever since she lost her faith. Very sad, really."

"Harry, did Mrs. Barlow seem troubled to you?"

"No. Didn't seem lost, either."

"My opinion, as well, Mr. Vander Walle. What makes you certain she 'is a troubled woman', 'a veritable lost soul'?"

"Well, I mean, I don't know her all—"

"Come now, Mr. Vander Walle. She was your pastor. You are church treasurer and have been for quite some time. I'm willing to wager you know her quite well. So based on your years of observation, what makes you think she's troubled and lost and therefore no credence should be given to what she's told us?"

"The exact same reason you mentioned: I've observed her behavior for a long time. Was I intimate with her? No. Are we friends? No. I'm not sure Mrs. Barlow has friends. However, I have observed her and my observations tell me, since losing her faith, she is an unstable and volatile woman. You've heard about her disgraceful behavior and her threats to kill her husband?"

"Yes."

"Well, there you have it."

Tina said nothing. Simply drummed her fingers on the desk.

Vander Walle took a sip of gin.

Tina stopped drumming her fingers and asked, "Why would Naomi Frame make an accusation that would eventually cause her to lose her job if there wasn't some grain of truth to it?"

"I don't know. You'll have to ask her."

"What did you think of Reverend Gary Barlow?"

"I liked him. His death is a tragedy, a disaster actually, for the church. There are those who don't see this. I'm trusting they will in time."

"What was his plan that had you and others in an uproar?"

Vander Walle smiled, took a sip of gin, swirled the liquid in the glass, and took another sip. "He wanted to tie church membership to acts of genuine service. One act of service a year to begin with. Not throw money at something, but a genuine act of human to human service."

Tina stood. "Thank you for your time, Mr. Vander Walle."

He finished his gin, stood, and said, "I'm glad I could be of help."

I saw him out and returned to my desk. Tina was still standing. A scowl on her face.

"Well?"

"He's a liar. As certain as I'm standing here, he was on intimate terms with Celeste and, together, they got Naomi fired."

"But that doesn't mean he killed Gary Barlow, nor does it provide Celeste with an alibi."

"No, it doesn't. Not by force, anyway. But I am very tempted to camp outside his doorstep with an IMSI-catcher and listen to what he has to tell us that he doesn't want to tell us."

I was amused. The Boss was talking about working. This case must be truly getting under her skin.

14

BUT JESUS NEVER WEPT

Monday Supper, 10 February

BRODIGAN DIDN'T ANSWER MY CALL AND BEA CHEATED. SHE WENT TO Byerly's and brought home roast chicken, deli coleslaw, pasta salad, and two take and bake pizzas. One of the pizzas had just come out of the oven when she called us for supper.

We sat down at the dinner table. Tina took a slice of pizza, this first one was pepperoni, and poured herself a glass of zinfandel. Bea took a slice of pizza, too, and poured a Schell's beer into a glass. I opted for a chicken leg, coleslaw, pasta salad, and a glass of California Gewürztraminer.

"So you do eat meat," Tina said.

"Yes, I do."

"I was beginning to think Gwen had made a convert out of you."

"Not yet. I'm an ovo-lacto-carno vegetarian."

"Huh. Not much carno left."

I took another chicken leg. "There. You happy?"

Bea was giggling. "You two are so funny."

Tina had a slight smile showing. "Glad you find us entertaining and thanks for supper, by the way."

Bea pulled the pizza slice away from her mouth. "You're welcome."

Business is rarely discussed outside of the office. Tina is a stickler for keeping work out of her life. Yes, that is correct. Tina doesn't like to work. She should have married the Prince of Monaco when he was available. Since she didn't, she has to work. The rules, though, are very strict. Like talking business when we are eating. Only under the direst of circumstances is it allowed. I only mention all of this because of what Tina said next.

"We need to pry open Celeste. Get her to stop dancing around the mulberry bush."

The forkful of pasta salad stopped in mid-air, half-way to my mouth. We were experiencing dire circumstances. Was the situation really that bad? She apparently thought so. I let the fork continue on its journey.

After chewing and swallowing. I asked, "Any ideas?"

"No. Not really."

"Why don't we just turn over what we have to the police and let the county attorney have her arrested."

The timer rang and Bea left, coming back shortly with the other pizza. A meat lover's special. Currying extra favor with the boss.

Tina was thoughtful. She picked up a slice of fresh, hot pizza, took a bite out of it, chewed, swallowed, and said, "We don't have to give them anything. They're good at routine, get sloppy sometimes, but generally they're good. If there is something with which to hang Celeste, they'll find it. Then we go to work to unhang her. She might be more cooperative when the noose is around her neck."

A forkful of pasta was on its way to my mouth and I put it on hold. "She might. Although if we blew up her story about Rhinelander, she might decide to cooperate."

Tina cocked her head to the side. "Possibly. Rhinelander's a dodge and at the end of the day I don't think that will move her. The police have undoubtedly gone over footage from the hotel's security camera's and already know the general features of who visited her room."

"They'd also know if and when she left," I said.

"Unless she was in disguise," Tina replied. She ate a bite of pizza and continued, "On the Sunny Day website, one has to be a member to see the good stuff and to be a member one has to apply and be approved. One can't even book an escort without being approved."

"Correct."

"Once approved, one then pays more money in order to sign up for the membership level of his choice."

"Correct again."

"I'm wondering. Celeste obviously likes you, Harry. She's offered you discounts and—"

Bea put down her glass of beer. "What? Celeste wants you to have sex with her?"

I was in for it and knew it. "Babe, I haven't—"

"Am I not pleasing you?" Bea was clearly put out.

"No, it's not that at all. Of course you are. For some reason—"

Tina came to my rescue. "Celeste is a business woman. For some reason she likes Harry and thinks you're cute, Bea, and is of the opinion the two of you will make her money and in the process you'll make yourselves money. What I was going to suggest was that maybe Harry should take her up on her offer and try to get a reduced rate for her site so we can scope it out from the inside. But your husband's a prude, Bea, and—"

Bea looked at me, then turned to Tina. "I don't think Harry's a prude. I mean, just the other night he—"

"Okay, Bea," Tina interrupted, "I believe you."

"Yeah, I mean I wanted—"

"Bea, I don't need a blow by blow of your sex life. I believe you. I take it back. Harry's not a prude."

Tina's face was as red as her hair. I couldn't help but smirk. Bea got her to blush. I love it.

Taking a deep breath, Tina continued. "Anyway, I was

thinking it might be worth our while to see her empire from the inside. But maybe not."

Bea took a sip of beer. She'd settled down and suddenly got a thoughtful look on her face. "What happens if you're not approved?"

"Don't know," Tina said. "I didn't see anything on the site that addressed that situation." She looked at me and I shrugged in response.

"I don't get it," Bea said. "Why would someone have to go through all that bother just to get an escort?"

"Don't know," Tina said around a bite of pizza.

"My guess," I volunteered, "is to make sure the customers can pay. The sign-up fee is, in reality, a non-refundable application fee."

"What is to prevent someone who is turned down from blowing the whistle?" Bea asked.

"Good question," Tina said, "Maybe no one's turned down. What did the premium level cost, Harry?"

"Twenty-five grand for the Platinum Membership. Not something your average blue-collar worker would pay."

Tina was thoughtful, ate a bite of pizza, then said, "So why the extra step of filling out a form for vetting. Just seems like overkill to me. If they can pay twenty-five thousand dollars, they can probably afford an escort."

"Maybe we ought to ask Celeste," I said.

Tina nodded. "Maybe we should. Unless the whole point of the vetting is to get their financial information to begin with. Maybe the sex empire is just a ruse for an extortion ring."

The doorbell rang. I got up muttering, "Who could that be?", and went to the door. There on our doorstep was Lieutenant Cal Swenson. I threw the door open.

"Come on in, Cal. Get out of the cold."

"Thanks, Harry. Am I interrupting anything?"

"No. We're having supper. Join us."

"Thanks, but I'm good."

He followed me into the dining room.

"Hi Tina, Bea."

"Hi, Cal!" Bea exclaimed.

"Have something to eat, Cal," Tina said.

"Maybe a slice of pizza," he replied.

Bea got up and took his coat. He sat and picked up a slice of meat lover's.

"I have good and bad news and they're the same news," he said before taking a bite of the pizza.

"Go ahead," Tina said.

He swallowed pizza, took a deep breath, let it out, and said, "Someone shot Celeste Barlow."

"Oh, my God," Bea said.

Tina let out a sigh. "Is she…?"

"She's still alive. The doctors don't hold out a lot of hope, though. Someone put three .32 caliber bullets into her. Probably why she's still breathing. A larger caliber and she'd be in the morgue."

"She was home alone?" I asked.

"Yes. We tracked her children down at her mother's."

"Feingold know?" Tina asked.

"Nelson called and left a message." He took another bite of pizza, chewed, and swallowed. "Guess that means she probably didn't off her husband. Although it could be she did and was shot by someone seeking revenge."

"Or by someone who thought she had," Tina said.

Cal nodded.

Tina continued. "Or she could have been shot for an entirely unrelated reason."

"Yeah, that too," Cal said. "In any event, I'm thinking she's not our number one suspect anymore."

"Anyone see anything?" I asked.

"Next door neighbor heard the shots. He was out walking his dog, but was several houses away and didn't get a good look at anything. Saw a dark shape run from Barlow's front door to a car and the car take off down the street. He ran, found the front door open and Celeste lying in the entry way. He called 911."

"Good news and bad news all rolled into one, as you said." Tina looked grim.

Bea sniffed. She was quietly crying. I went to her and put my arms around her.

No one said anything. I think we were trying to absorb what it all meant. The first one to break the silence was Tina.

"For whom does the bell toll?"

Bea, with her tear-soaked voice, answered, "It tolls for thee."

To which Tina added, "But Jesus never wept."

15

THE MAN WITH THE CARD

Monday Night: 8 to 9, 10 February

CAL LEFT SHORTLY AFTER TINA'S OBSERVATION ABOUT JESUS. LOIS Gorman rang our doorbell promptly at eight. I had five photographs of Ben Franklin on greenish paper all ready for her. I ushered her into the Inner Sanctum, made introductions, guided her to the oxblood wingback, and then sat at my desk.

Tina wasted no time. "Ms. Gorman, can you describe to me the east Asian man who wanted to see Reverend Gary Barlow a month or so ago?"

"How do you—"

Tina waved the question away. "It's my job to know things. I repeat. Can you describe the man to me?"

"Oh, that's right. You hired that nice man, David. Well, let me see, the man who came to see Reverend Barlow wasn't overly tall. Certainly less than six feet. He wore a suit in navy, a white shirt, and no tie. He was young. I'd guess he wasn't over thirty. His English was good. Let's see." She paused and reflected. "Short, black hair. Wingtip shoes. Overcoat was also navy. It was open when he came in. His voice was not loud."

"Were his facial features more like this picture or this one?" Tina asked.

"The first one."

"What did he say?"

"He asked to speak with Reverend Barlow. I told him the Reverend was not in. He gave me his card and asked that I give it to the Reverend. Then he left."

"Did he have any tattoos?"

"None that I could see."

"What was on the business card?"

"Chinese or Japanese symbols."

"Nothing else?"

"Nothing."

"He never came back?"

"No."

"Did Reverend Barlow have a reaction when he saw the card?"

"He saw it the next day and asked me just about the same questions you just asked."

"Was he agitated, scared, curious?"

"If anything, I'd say he was perhaps scared."

"Thank you, Ms. Gorman. You've been most helpful."

I escorted Lois back out to the cold, cruel world. She left with five hundred more dollars in her pocket than she had when she arrived. Hopefully the money made braving the cold and the traffic worth it. Back in the office I looked at Tina.

"Was it worth five Cs?" I asked.

"I think so. She picked the picture of the man with Japanese facial features."

"So?"

"Seppuku, Harry."

"Ah, seppuku. Is the Japanese fellow our murderer?"

"Possibly. I need to know what David's people have discovered. Also, find out if the church has security cameras." She paused. "I suppose Feingold will call in the morning."

"Probably."

"The key is seppuku, Harry. Have Gwen and Ed come in, too."

She got up and left the office and I was left with trying to figure out the significance of seppuku and how it fit into all of this. I didn't spend a lot of time on it. After all, the recipe was missing a few ingredients.

I texted David, asked him for a report, and wrote a note to myself to check on the church's security system in the morning.

With Celeste heading for that land beyond the Jordan, I didn't see much sense in pursuing any of this. Of course, Tina would say she isn't dead yet and therefore she was still our client. And so long as she is our client we're going to continue to work on her behalf.

Given that, I'm still not sure where seppuku fits into all of this. I think it's a given there is a message there. Also obvious is that the good Reverend Barlow did not cut himself open. But what lock seppuku is the key to, I'm still trying to figure out. What I didn't have to figure out was how to text Gwen and Ed.

16

PHEBE

Tuesday Morning, 11 February

Feingold got to us first with a phone call at seven after eight. I'd been in the kitchen all of two minutes. Didn't even have the tea on.

"Good morning, Mr. Feingold."

"You heard about Celeste?"

"We heard."

"I'm keeping you on the case. Just don't do anything until we see which way she goes."

"I'll let Tina know."

"Thanks." And I was left with a dial tone in my ear.

Still employed. That was good. Sit around and do nothing. That's also kind of good. Enjoying the sweetness of doing nothing and getting paid for it. I guess I could get used to that. I started making tea and Bea joined me.

"Will they still have the funeral?" she asked.

"Don't know. Good question. Why do you ask?"

"Just wondering. Those poor children."

"It's a major bummer, that's for sure. Dad brutally murdered and now Mom shot and clinging to life by a thread."

"Do you think they're connected?"

"Don't know. The modus operandi says 'no'. Then again maybe the killer likes variety. Spices up life."

"Harry, you shouldn't be so flip."

"Sorry, Babe. I guess being flip helps to keep a little distance. Reduces the chance for burnout."

The look on her face told me she wasn't buying it. I shrugged and focused on breakfast preparations.

Tina entered the kitchen. She was wearing a black skirt suit with wide pleats to the skirt, white blouse, navy bowtie, and her red hair was swept up and fixed in a bun on top of her head.

"Good morning," she said. "Tea ready?"

Something was up. Tina is never, and I mean never, that talkative in the morning. At least before breakfast.

"Tea will be ready in a few minutes," I said.

"Okay," she replied, then turned to Bea, "call the Collins residence and find out if they are having the funeral today."

Bea said, "Consider it done," and left the kitchen, in the direction of the office.

Since we were talking business, I said, "Feingold called. He's keeping us on the case, but doesn't want us doing anything until we know which direction Celeste is going."

Tina nodded, and departed for the dining room; which left me in the kitchen to get the breakfast ready. Tea, toast, jam, soft-boiled eggs and bacon were on the morning menu. Bea returned in short order, carrying the newspaper. She set the paper down and helped me finish breakfast preparations.

We carried the food to the dining room where the princess had her nose in her iPad. I poured tea, while Bea retrieved the newspaper and brought it to the dining room. We each took a section, and the morning ritual was underway.

Without looking up, Tina said, "Well?"

"No funeral," Bea answered. "They're going to wait and see if Celeste lives or not."

Tina nodded.

I couldn't help but think they were merely postponing the funeral in the hope of getting a two-for-one special. With no funeral, Tina could probably change into something other than black. That she was wearing black in the first place was something.

Out of the blue, Tina said, "Did you wash your hands? I didn't hear any water running."

By now you may have detected Tina has a phobia about newspapers. What with printer's ink coming off on your hands and God knows how many germs might be on a newspaper because of all the people handling it, in her mind it's a wonder humanity has survived at all. And the funniest part of it is that she's not consistent. Some days she'll rag on us and other days not.

Bea said, "Yes."

I spelled "liar" with my egg yolk.

Bea added, "I used a disinfectant wipe."

Tina didn't reply. I wasn't sure she was buying the story. She didn't pursue it, so maybe she did. Or maybe her query was merely force of habit.

My curiosity was piqued, so I asked, "You were going to go to the funeral today?"

Without looking up from the iPad, she said, "Weren't you?"

"Hadn't thought about it."

She looked at me. "He was our client."

"We don't go to all or even most of our former client's funerals."

She shook her head and resumed communion with the iPad.

When the morning meal was safely stowed under our belts, we moved on to the office to await the arrival of David, Gwen, and Ed. On the way, though, Tina made us wash our hands and watched while we did so. One will get you ten, Tina didn't believe Bea. Probably also explains why I didn't see her eat anything.

In the office, Tina and I sat at our desks and Bea stretched out on the chesterfield.

"Okay, I get that seppuku is out of the ordinary and we need to look at it," I said, "but traditional Japanese seppuku isn't done that way."

"You're right, Harry, it isn't," Tina replied. "This was clearly a variation on the theme, undoubtedly as a taunting of Barlow's faith. The cross cut, forming the patibulum of the cross, was a correct seppuku cut. What the murderer added was the cut beginning at the navel to form the stipes of the cross. Omitted from the ritual was the decapitation, which leads me to believe the murderer wanted Barlow to suffer."

"That's horrible!" Bea exclaimed.

"Murder is horrible," Tina replied. "Our job is to discover who did this and why and bring him or her to justice. The main clue before us is the manner in which Barlow was executed."

"Executed?" That one threw me for a loop.

"Yes, Harry, executed. Seppuku was a traditional form of capital punishment in Japan. Which also leads me to believe we are dealing with someone who is either Japanese or a Japanophile."

The doorbell rang and Bea got up to answer the door. When she returned, David Nagasawa was with her. Greetings were exchanged and David took a seat in the oxblood wingback.

Before David was able to begin his report, the doorbell rang. Bea left to answer the door and when she returned both Gwen Poisson and Ed Hafner were with her. Greetings were exchanged and they took seats on the chesterfield.

I asked Bea to bring tea and cucumber water. I noticed Ed had a paper cup of coffee. Tempting fate, he was, daring to bring it into the Inner Sanctum.

"Thank you for coming," Tina said. "David, I'd like to hear your report first."

"I've had a couple friends in San Francisco working on uncovering anything connected to Reverend Barlow's missing year."

Bea was back and distributed beverages. David continued.

"Our greatest problem is time. Barlow was there twenty-five years ago and going by an alias. My friends have circulated his high school picture and college yearbook photos and have found four people who say they recall him. Unfortunately, they didn't know him well and only two could even remember his name. One knew him only as Garth. The other as Garth Betts. In twenty-five years, people move, people die, and people forget. They can keep looking if you want."

"Tell your people to hold off for now."

"Will do, Miss Wright."

"What have you found on Celeste's sister, Gwen?"

"Not a whole lot. Divorced five years ago. Has two kids. After the divorce settlement, the upheaval in the financial markets, and her own lack of money management, she's basically broke. Or was. About eight months ago she started doing very well in the money department, but no one knows where the cash is coming from and she's not saying anything specific. Says she's gotten help from Celeste and some investments have paid off. Trouble is, I can't find any investments."

"She have a good relationship with Celeste?"

"Good enough. They appear to be close, but not exceptionally so."

"In what way?"

"It took some digging, but I found a couple high school friends who said Celeste had the bad habit of stealing Nicole's boyfriends."

"Really?"

"That's what they said. Created some bad blood apparently. Things seem to have settled down since then, but one never knows. Those old sibling rivalries have a way of lingering."

"That they do." Tina cast a look in my direction.

"What are you looking at me for? I never did anything to you."

"We'll talk about it later."

Ed drank coffee, Gwen had a knowing smirk on her face, and David shook his head.

"There'll be nothing to talk about. Geez."

Tina went back to the interview. "Nicole have a love interest?"

"None I could find."

The Boss leaned back in her chair, tented her fingers under her chin. She stayed that way for a minute or two, then leaned forward and said to Gwen, "Something's not right there. Keep watching her. Eavesdrop and hack her if necessary."

Tina was playing the cowgirl again. She gets like this sometimes when she's frustrated. Usually she just pulls out altogether. Goes on vacation. I think with Celeste stiff-arming her, Tina decided to take out her frustrations on Celeste's sister.

"Anything else, Tina?" Gwen asked. Gwen's the only one of the three freelancers who can get away with calling her "Tina".

"No. Just find out what the mystery is all about. I'm sick and tired of the mystery in that family. What do you have for me, Ed?"

Ed set his cup down, cleared his throat, and began. "Bridger Randolph Collins was born in '65 and is forty-eight. Married for twenty years. Wife's name is Stacy. They have two kids: Bridger, Junior, is sixteen and Stacy, Junior, is ten. He's rolling in the dough. Has a place in North Oaks and another in the province of Como, Italy. Owns his own Learjet 60. That's thirteen mil worth of airplane. He's flying in from Milan, making it a three-day hop. Should be here Thursday.

"Not a nice guy. Talked with some former classmates and a couple people he's had business dealings with. Mom thinks the world of him. Apparently Dad did, too. His sisters, not so much."

Gwen interrupted. "Actually, I'd say Nicole can't stand him. In her words, 'He didn't do a goddamn thing for me when I was going through my divorce and afterwards wouldn't even give me shit on a plate when I needed money.'"

Ed nodded and took a sip of his coffee.

Tina looked at her desktop, chin resting on steepled index fingers. After a few minutes, she took a deep breath, exhaled, and looked at the three freelancers.

She said, "Thank you for the information you've gathered. I assume you've heard that Celeste was shot." Their nods were confirmation they'd heard the news. "For now, David and Ed, I have no further need of your services. Please write up your reports and give your expense sheets to Harry. Feingold has put us on hold; although, Gwen, you'll continue checking on Nicole, as we discussed. I want that piece of the puzzle behind us should Feingold give us the green light to continue."

I walked with the three out to the door, bid them farewell, and returned to the Inner Sanctum. Bea followed me and resumed her previous position on the chesterfield.

To Tina, I said, "Now what?"

"Call Elena Urban. Have her send a report and expense sheet and thank her for her time."

"Still want to meet with Phebe? She has an appointment for eleven."

"Yes. She might be a Japanophile."

I used my desk phone to call Elena. She didn't answer, so I left a message with the vital information and followed up with an email. The time was close to eleven. Bea went out to her desk, I drank tea, and Tina picked up *The Art Forgers Handbook*. Thus the minutes ticked by until the doorbell rang.

A moment later, Bea ushered in Phebe Vander Walle. She was a tall and thin woman. Everything about her was expensive. Her dress, jewelry, shoes, hair, perfume, all indicated she had money to burn and did so regularly. Bea made introductions and I guided our visitor to the oxblood wingback.

Tina looked at her and asked, "Do you own a jet?"

"I beg your pardon?"

"Do you you own a jet?"

"I don't know what this is about—"

"Harry, do the Vander Walles own a jet?"

"No, they don't."

Tina nodded.

"Your assistant implied you have information which compromises my alibi. What is it?"

"Are you a Japanophile, Mrs. Vander Walle?" Tina asked.

"A what?"

"A Japanophile. I lover of things Japanese. Are you? Do you?"

"What kind of a detective are you?"

"A very good one. Are you Japanophile?"

"No."

"Do you own a Japanese car?"

"I own a Lexus. Is that Japanese?"

"It is. Why?"

"Why what?"

"Why do you own a Lexus if you aren't a Japanophile?"

"I like the looks and they're supposed to be very reliable. I like that."

Tina sat back in her chair drummed her fingers on the left arm. She'd lost interest in Phebe, who was obviously not Japanese and equally obviously not a Japanophile. Besides, I had my doubts she could perform seppuku. Might get something distasteful on her hands.

"Why did you want Reverend Gary Barlow to leave the church?"

"I've talked to the police. Are you going to tell me what you heard or not?"

"We've had a person tell us he saw you at the Barlow residence the night Reverend Barlow was murdered."

"The person is lying. I was nowhere near the Barlow residence. James and I were dining at Lord Fletcher's."

"I suppose someone can corroborate?"

"Of course. We had reservations. William, the Maitre d', can corroborate."

"Thank you, Mrs. Vander Walle. You've been most helpful."

Phebe stood. "I did not like Reverend Barlow's vision for the church. And it's true I wanted him to leave. He was a nice man and I'm sorry he died such a horrible death. I just wanted him to leave. I didn't want him dead. And I certainly didn't kill him."

Tina stood. "I understand. Good day."

Phoebe left and Tina announced she'd be in the music room.

Bea was at her desk, which left me alone in the Inner Sanctum. I walked over to Tina's desk and sat in her chair. Tina was preoccupied with seppuku. I had my own preoccupation. Namely, how did Celeste send an email when the police had their computers? Did she have a smart phone for personal use? If so, then she could have used her phone to send an email. Maybe she just had a primitive cell phone. If so, then I was back to my initial question. Quite obviously, I needed to make a couple phone calls. I picked up Tina's desk phone and began punching numbers.

17

STEPPIN' ON CLOUDS

Tuesday Afternoon, 11 February

AGAIN, I FOUND MYSELF STANDING IN THE BARLOW HOME. Although how much longer the house would actually be a home for the Barlow family was up for grabs.

My phone call to Cal informed me the police had retrieved Celeste's cell phone. An old flip model. He was also generous enough to answer my question about Barlow's church's security cameras. They had them and they were the new digital kind.

My second phone call to the Collins's residence resulted in me meeting Genevieve at the Barlow house. Mrs. Collins had decided to loan me a key for the duration of the investigation. Genevieve gave me the key, headed back to the Collins's place, while I let myself in to investigate the Barlow home.

I took in the entry. Nothing special. A small area with tiled floor and a coat closet. The little entry way functioned as a hub from which one could proceed to the living room, kitchen, or upstairs. I hung up my coat in the closet and put my hat on the shelf. The living room was just a few steps away. I took them and was once again in that relatively sterile room.

The pictures hanging on the walls appeared to be real paintings. The one hanging directly over the fireplace was a garish splash of color portraying a street scene. The artist's name was in Cyrillic. Russian. On either side were smaller paintings by Lois Mooney. A contemporary Midwestern regional artist, who paints ethereal dusky landscapes. Quite a contrast between the Mooney paintings and the Russian.

Over the sofa, which faced the fireplace, was a painting, highly stylized, yet it remained understandable as a house on a street. The painting was by Charles Burchfield. Now that one was probably worth some money. I wasn't sure I'd have it in my living room, if I had one, but as far as paintings go it was pretty good.

I looked them over, noticed nothing unusual, and turned my attention to the rest of the room. There were plenty of places to hide things. The question was, would she hide anything in this room? My conclusion was, no, she wouldn't. Too easy to get caught in the act of retrieving or hiding.

The living room opened onto the dining room and I passed on into that room. A quick look around and I felt it unlikely Celeste would hide anything in the dining room. Again, too easy to get caught. What did catch my eye, though, where the three paintings on the wall. A landscape by H. R. Fish and flanking, on either side, landscapes by Charles S. Graham: "Garden of the Gods" and "Lone Figure in a Valley". And what caught my eye about them is Tina has made copies of all three in the past. These however did not bear her "J. Wright after____" signature.

Smart phones are a wonderful invention. I accessed the web and searched. It didn't take me long to find the paintings and info about the artists. Both are known Northern California artists from the late 1800s and early 1900s. Of additional interest was that Graham was a member of the Bohemian Club, as was Sterling.

Another connection to Barlow in San Francisco. Or so it seemed. I did some calculating. Barlow had departed San Francisco fifteen years before Tina arrived. I looked at the paintings. Probably just coincidence.

My best chance would be upstairs and specifically Celeste's

room. I walked back out to the entryway, took the stairs to the second floor, and made my way to Celeste's bedroom. I stood in the doorway and took in the room before entering. Once inside, by the dust outline on her desk, I could tell where her computer had sat. There was a painting on the wall over the desk and another over the headboard of her bed.

Thanks to Tina's revelation in the Copley murder, I examined each painting and both fit the bill. I took them off the wall and laid them facedown on the bed. The one that had been on the wall by the bed was on the heavy side. Too heavy if you asked me. I got out my pocket knife and carefully took off the back. Money. Piles of it. Celeste's secret stash. I put the panel back where it belonged and rehung the painting.

The one she had over the desk I gave a good once over and discovered a removable panel in the side, just behind the frame. I took off the panel and felt inside the opening. Then very carefully extracted an iPad mini. I turned it on and of course she had it password protected.

Most people write down passwords or combinations, because our memories aren't that good. And even though the iPad password was short, I was willing to bet she'd written it down. Just in case she forgot it. After all, we have so many passwords to keep track of nowadays. So I started looking for the passcode.

Nothing in the little pocket in which the iPad had been hiding. Next, the desk drawers. I pulled them out and saw nothing on the inside, nor on the outside. I looked behind the desk and under the desk. Nothing there. I took apart her nightstands. Nothing. I looked behind the headboard. Bingo. A little sticky note with four numbers on it. I tapped those numbers on the iPad and voilà! I had access. Now what was I looking for?

I asked myself, "Harry, if you were a prostitute how would you keep track of appointments and regulars?" And in answer, I said, "Well, I think I'd use the Calendar, Contacts, and Reminders."

I started with the Calendar and looked at the date Reverend

Gary was murdered. And there it was. A name, "Flinny", followed by a number six. Hm. "Flinny". I'd guess that to be a nickname. Next I checked the Reminders app. Bingo. "Meeting and dinner — Flinders Nussbaum." And finally the Contacts app. Yes, indeed. We were in like Flinders. His name, address, phone, and email.

"Harry, my man," I said out loud, "you just blew this thing wide open."

I hung the picture back on the wall, copied the passcode, and put the sticky back. A lively trot down the stairs to the entryway, where I donned my coat and hat, then exited, locked up, and nearly ran to the Harrymobile for the drive home. Needless to say, I was steppin' on clouds.

18

NUSSBAUM

Tuesday night, 11 February

I GOT HOME IN TIME FOR SUPPER. BEA HAD MADE CHILI AND A TOSSED salad. I decided to forgo wine. We'd have beer with supper: Schell's Pilsner for Bea and Sam Adams Cream Stout for Tina and me. We sat down and Tina started a spoon of chili to her mouth. Before it got there I said, "We are in possession of Sunny Day's iPad Mini and I know where some of her cash is."

The spoon paused, Tina uttered a "very good", and the spoon completed its journey.

The conversation, however, segued to the death of Shirley Temple, the trouble in the Ukraine, and the Olympics. When supper was over and the dishes cleaned up, we adjourned to the office to discuss the iPad. Tina sat at her desk, I at mine, and Bea stretched out on the chesterfield.

I held up the little tablet. "This is Sunny Day's office. She has her calendar here and her records. What's more, we now know who she was with while someone was killing her husband. Whoever Flinders Nussbaum is, that is who she's protecting. We have his address, phone, and email."

Tina had a big smile on her face. "Invite Mr. Nussbaum for a visit."

I checked the time. Seven-thirty. Not too late. I picked up my phone and dialed his number. On the fourth ring he answered with a simple "Yes?"

"Mr. Nussbaum, I'm Harry Wright, from Wright Investigations. Celeste Barlow's attorney hired us to help find her husband's murderer and keep her out of jail."

"How did you get this number?" His voice sounded funny. He must have turned on some kind of voice altering software.

"Your name is in the iPad Mini I'm holding in my hand."

"What do you want?"

"My sister, the famous investigator, Justinia Wright, would like to speak with you."

"What's your address?"

I gave it to him and he replied he'd be at our place by eight-thirty. A dial tone replaced his voice.

"He'll be here by eight-thirty," I said.

Tina smiled. "I'm willing to wager he's her partner in the sex empire."

"Which means he probably won't tell us much."

"True, Harry, true. My guess is, he probably wants to gain possession of the iPad. If I'm correct, he might end up telling us quite a bit in exchange for the device."

"Wouldn't he have one?" Bea asked.

"Most likely," Tina replied. "However, he doesn't need the iPad for its information. He needs it to keep it out of undesirable hands."

"Oh, sure. That makes sense. But we're trying to help Celeste."

"That is true. Even so, I'm sure he doesn't want the business to see the light of day and therefore wants the device. With Celeste's iPad in his hands, no one will be any wiser as to what is going on, unless they stumble on the website. And even there, she was careful not to have her face showing. Given the size of her empire, we could be talking many millions of dollars here."

"Wow."

"Sex is big business, Babe," I added.

Bea giggled. "I might have to start charging you, Harry."

Tina laughed. "You shouldn't have let her give away all that money, Big Brother."

"Huh. Guess not."

The clock ticked away and at eight-eighteen the doorbell rang. I went to get it. When I opened the door I saw before me a large man, easily standing six-two, somewhere in his forties. By large, I don't mean fat. I mean broad shouldered, rugged, lumberjack-type.

His voice rumbled like a freight train. "I'm Flinders Nussbaum."

"I'm Harry Wright."

I motioned for him to come in, which he did. But he didn't just come in, he strode in. He took off his mid-calf length brown wool coat and brown leather gloves, putting them in a coat pocket. I hung the coat on a peg by the door, while he removed his over-shoes and left them on the floor beneath his coat.

"Follow me," I said and led him into the Inner Sanctum.

I made introductions all around and had him sit in the oxblood oversized wingback at the far corner of Tina's desk. The chair wasn't oversized for him.

"Nice office," he rumbled.

"Thank you," Tina purred.

I thought, what's up with that? Truly, Nussbaum was a hunk. Maybe he's been in the porn or escort business himself. He did have something of that Peter North look. But for Tina to be purring? Sheesh.

"How much do you want for it?" he asked. He wasn't wasting any time beating around the bush.

Tina laughed. "Mr. Nussbaum, only my paintings and my time are for purchase. Are you interested?" The purr had returned on the last sentence.

He looked her up and down. At least what he could see that

wasn't covered by the desk. "Perhaps," he replied, "but what I want for sure is the iPad. Celeste's iPad."

"My guess is we are on the same side," Tina said, "after all, Celeste's lawyer hired us to exonerate her, or find the murderer of her husband."

"I take it you want to hold on to the iPad."

"I do, Mr. Nussbaum, because it provides an alibi for my client."

"One she doesn't want you to use."

"As of the last time we spoke with her, that's true."

"So, it seems to me," Nussbaum said, "you are left with the option of trying to find the killer."

Tina shook her head. "Not so. I don't have to follow her request."

Fear flitted across Nussbaum's face. "You wouldn't turn the iPad over to the police, would you?"

"Probably not. I don't want to get her off one charge only to have another brought against her. I'm sure you feel the same as I do: the sex laws in this country are antiquated, based on an ethical system the majority no longer subscribes to."

He smiled and for the first time appeared to relax. He reached into his suit coat pocket and pulled out a cigar. "I smell cigar in here. Do you mind?"

"Not at all," Tina said. "Be my guest."

He got out his clipper and cut the end of the cigar. Tina reached for her humidor.

"Oh, please, try this."

Tina cocked an eyebrow.

"It is a Romeo y Julieta from Cuba." He stood and held out the cigar for her. "Have you ever had a Cuban cigar?"

"In Europe."

"Well, then, you know. What do you smoke?"

"Muniemaker Longs."

Nussbaum raised his eyebrows, returned to his seat and took another cigar from his pocket. That he didn't wrinkle his nose, I thought showed he had tremendous self-control. Don't get me wrong. I'm sure his cigar was on the whole better than what Tina usually smokes. But Muniemaker is a darn good cigar, even if it is machine made. None of that tobacco sheet crap. They use real leaves.

Reminds me of the story about Mark Twain. His guests always complained about how rank his cigars were. So one day he bought several boxes of a premium brand, dumped the cigars out and put his cigars into the premium boxes. After dinner, he handed out the cigars and his guests were effusive in their praise of his improved taste. Of course it was Twain who had the last laugh.

Once they had the cigars going and I had turned on the fan so we who weren't smoking would be able to breathe, Tina asked if he cared for a drink.

"Scotch and water?" Nussbaum replied.

I informed him all we had was Grant's.

"Grant's is okay. No water and a brandy snifter."

Huh. The Grant's was good enough for a snifter. That surprised me.

"Coming right up," I said without any hint of a purr.

I left and went to the kitchen, poured a double into a brandy snifter, poured myself a Drambuie, and returned to the office. Tina was having madeira. I handed Nussbaum his drink and returned to my desk.

"Want anything, Babe?"

Bea shook her head.

Our guest swirled the whiskey, nosed, swirled, and nosed again. Finally he took a sip.

Tina drank madeira and said, "Now it's my turn to ask questions."

"What do you want to know?" Nussbaum replied.

"Why is Celeste protecting you?"

"Not me specifically. She's protecting her business. I happen to be her accountant, business manager, and web designer. Her Man Friday, so to speak."

Tina smiled. *Probably because I'm her Man Friday.* "What happens to the business if Celeste dies?"

"Her sister becomes Sunny Day."

"Nicole is in the business with her?"

"Very much so."

"Why?"

"Money, mostly. Her divorce and the recession wiped her out. Celeste took her in as a partner."

Well, I'll be doggone. A family internet brothel empire. Maybe now I have indeed heard everything.

Tina too was absorbing the info Nussbaum had volunteered. She closed her eyes and leaned back in her chair, then came forward and opened them. "What's to prevent Nicole Collins from speeding up the inheritance?"

Now it was Nussbaum's turn. He raised his eyebrows and partially obscured his magnificently rugged forehead. He pursed his lips and looked for all the world as though this thought had never occurred to him. His eyebrows returned to where they belonged and his lips unpursed. He took a sip of scotch.

"I suppose nothing, Miss Wright. Except they are very close and I just can't imagine it."

"Okay, for sake of argument, let's say sister Nicole is horrified at the attack on Celeste. Who do you think might have wanted Celeste dead?" Tina wasn't purring now.

"Not I," Nussbaum said. "I make a half-million tax free dollars a year. I know a good thing when I see it. The work I do for Celeste is easier than making porn flicks and there's no chance of disease."

So he was in the porn industry. The old gut is still working.

Tina was undaunted. "Okay, not you. But who?"

"How would I know? To be honest, Miss Wright, it's a real pisser. If you find the bastard or bitch, may I have a few minutes

alone with him or her? I used to box, you know. Was rather good."
He blew a cloud of smoke towards the ceiling.

She smiled and purred. "I'll think about it."

"I'm really sorry I can't help you. I can look over the client
database and forward names of those we've blacklisted. A few of
them are very nasty persons."

"That would be helpful."

I asked, "How much does the business make?"

"We gross a quarter to a third of a million each month. Business expenses are small, so it's mostly profit."

"That is a lot of money, Mr. Nussbaum," Tina said. "What do
Celeste and Nicole make?"

"Celeste gets sixty percent of the net and Nicole, forty."

Out of the blue, Bea asked, "How did you meet Mrs. Barlow?"

Nussbaum turned sideways to look at Bea. "I'd have to say
luck more than anything else brought us together. She needed a
webmaster and an accountant. I majored in accounting and
minored in web design. We met in a coffee shop. As I recall, she
was behind me and the line wasn't moving. We got to talking,
finally got our coffee, continued talking, exchanged phone
numbers, met again, and I joined her enterprise.

"I worked in the porn industry for three years after college
because I couldn't find an accounting job. I had orgasms to pay
my bills and pay off student loans, and did a little freelance web
design on the side. I have the physique that is in high demand for
porn, you know. Very attractive to gays as well. I'm straight, but
gay for pay got me more money. And it is all about the money,
even when you're having orgasms to earn it."

"Why didn't you stay in porn?" Bea asked.

"There was an AIDS scare and I decided I wanted none of that.
About the same time, the indie author movement began taking off
and all of these new authors needed websites and help with social
media. I was beginning to make more money from web development than porn. It was a good time to leave and I did. I moved to
Minneapolis, ended up meeting Celeste, and embarked on a new

career. She's a wonderful woman. I love her like a sister. This situation is for the shits, pardon my French."

Tina asked, "You ever meet Celeste's husband?"

"Yes, several times. He was a good man."

"You've been helpful, Mr. Nussbaum. We'll protect the iPad and you. For now."

Nussbaum stood. "Just find the person, will you?"

"We will," Tina assured him.

I escorted him to the door, we shook hands, and he left. I returned to the office.

"He's kind of stuck on himself," Bea said.

"That he is," Tina replied. "Makes me think of my friend F. Tennyson Jesse."

"Who's that?" Bea asked.

"She's not literally a friend," Tina said, and leaned back in her chair. "Dead now. She was a criminologist. Mrs. Jesse wrote, among other things, 'Vanity is the hallmark of the criminal,' and Mr. Nussbaum is certainly vain."

"Are you saying he did it?" Bea asked. "He's the killer?"

Tina shook her head. "I'm not saying he killed the Reverend Mr. Barlow or shot the Reverend Mrs. Barlow. I am saying he is a vain man and that vanity is the hallmark of the criminal."

Bea looked confused.

"That's okay, Babe. I don't get it either."

"Harry, what is there not to get?"

"Look, Tina, he either did the deed or he didn't."

"Not true at this point. We don't know if he did or didn't. All we know is that he is vain and so are criminals, especially murderers. He has plenty of motive, namely money. Perhaps he and Nicole decided to off Celeste for more money, a bigger cut of the pie. It wouldn't be the first time in history."

"Okay, Boss, where does that leave us?"

"It leaves us, my dear brother and sister-in-law, with a suspect. No more. No less. He has a motive. Nicole has a motive. Whether or not they did the deed remains to be seen."

Tina stood. "You two have a good night. I'm going to my room." The Great Detective left us.

"Well, Harry, I don't think finding the iPad helped a whole lot. It just gave us more suspects."

"Yeah. Isn't detective work fun?"

Clearly, we were no further ahead. If anything, we'd just made the case more complex. What wasn't so complex was Bea taking off her clothes and wanting to pretend we were making a porn vid.

19

FORGIVE YOURSELF

Wednesday Morning, 12 February

TINA DECIDED SHE AND I SHOULD PAY CELESTE A VISIT. BEA WAS LEFT to hold down the fort. When we got to the hospital, we found Celeste already had visitors. I recognized her mother and assumed the two children were the Barlow kids. As to the other woman, I took a wild guess that she was Celeste's sister. There was also a not so friendly man in blue outside the door. The public word was Celeste was in serious, yet stable, condition. Whatever that means. And being in the Intensive Care Unit, only family could see her. We took seats in the visitor's lounge.

"What do we do next, Tina?"

"I don't know, Harry. Feingold wants us to sit tight and I don't blame him. If Celeste dies, then it's all moot. On the other hand, if she lives then us sitting here twiddling our thumbs is a waste of time."

"We aren't exactly twiddling our thumbs. Gwen is still checking on Nicole."

"She is. If she finds something, we're good. If not, then at least we'll have a better idea who didn't do it."

"True."

Tina folded her hands behind her head. "Nussbaum and Nicole have powerful motives. Three to four million a year is a lot of money. If the cost of doing business, including Nussbaum's salary, is let's say twenty-five percent, then the sisters are pulling in at least two and a quarter million a year. That's a very hefty pay raise for Nussbaum and a not so insignificant one for Nicole. And all of it, tax free. Or relatively so. I can't imagine they aren't keeping cooked books in case the IRS comes knocking."

"Probably they do have books. Technically they are an escort business, not a whorehouse. Providing lonely and single businessmen and women a companion for the evening. If sex happens, well doggone it, people will be people."

Tina had a smirk on her face. "Sometimes you are so cynical. You are, though, correct. And then, she can always say she really doesn't have any business. Just a website with a lot of lookers or not so many. All the numbers can be cooked. Nevertheless, given what Nussbaum told us, they are pulling in some significant cash and with Celeste out of the way the two remaining people can get more of that cash in their pockets."

"Sounds like motive to me."

"It does indeed."

There was a lull after that, with neither one of us saying anything. Tina looked at her iPad and I read a small paperback of Coblentz's *Hidden World*. After a time she looked up and closed the cover on the tablet. "Harry, is there really any right and wrong?"

I closed the paperback on a finger. "Depends."

"On what?"

"What you believe."

"I'm talking about honest to goodness, incontrovertible right and wrong."

"And I'm saying what you believe determines if there is a categorical right and wrong or not."

I don't think she liked my answer. She was quiet and when she spoke, her voice was barely above a whisper. "I've done awful things in my life, Harry. I did them for a cause I believed in which I hoped might justify them and I hoped a merciful Jesus would forgive me. That's what Dad and Mom taught us. Jesus forgives sinners. Now I find out there never was a Jesus and, to be honest, I'm not sure the cause I believed in was all that good. If there is no justification for what I did and no forgiveness, how do I cope with what I did?"

"You have to forgive yourself. And then move on."

"What if I can't?" Her eyes looked as though they were about to spill tears.

"How have you managed for the past how many years?"

"Our upbringing, you know. I just assumed there was a Jesus and I had a safety net. Anytime, I could repent of my sins and be forgiven. Now I find out there is no Jesus. I have no safety net."

"Tina, no one *knows* if there was a Jesus or not. If believing there was a historical Jesus makes you feel better, then believe."

"Do you believe?"

"No. There is no outside, non-Christian, corroboration of his existence. Even the Quran, although not Christian, follows Christian tradition. It is not an independent witness. There is no proof, as I see it, Jesus ever existed."

"So how can *you* tell *me* to believe?"

"Because I think it is *all* a matter of belief."

"Everything?"

"Only what is, not viewed through some kind of filter or judgment, is real."

"Isn't that also a belief?"

"I suppose it is. We only see the world through what we can perceive. There is so much more out there. What we are aware of is really in our minds, limited by what we can sense. At times augmented by instruments. But even what they can measure is limited by our limitations. How do you know of that of which you can't possibly conceive? If the concept of God is true that he is totally other, then it is impossible for us to conceive of what God is. Which is why every myth anthropomorphizes God, so humans can have some manner of understanding and connection. And if true, then we still only know a part and not the whole. If believing in Jesus makes you feel better, then believe in him."

"Celeste's arguments on her blog are very convincing. I don't think I can anymore."

"Then you're going to have to forgive yourself and move on."

She nodded and wiped at her eyes. "I wouldn't have done any of it, had I known."

"Probably most of us can say that about some aspect of our lives. I certainly can."

"I suppose so."

"Why do you do detective work?"

"I want to help people. I want to see justice prevail."

"Then think of the job as penance for the people you didn't help."

"Yes. I suppose I can."

Tina stood and stretched. "Let's go down to Celeste's room."

We walked past the nurse's station to her room. We asked the cop on guard duty if we could speak to one of the family, explaining we were working with Celeste's attorney.

The man in blue, opened the door and checked with the people inside. In a moment, the woman I had earlier guessed to be Celeste's sister came out to speak with us. She bore a resemblance to Celeste, but was not anywhere near as attractive.

"Can I help you?" she asked.

"I'm Justinia Wright. I'm a private detective. Celeste's attorney, Harold Feingold, hired me. This is my brother and assistant, Harry."

"I'm Celeste's sister, Nicole. So what can I do for you?"

"We just wanted to find out how she is doing."

"She's alive. No change."

Tina nodded.

"Did you meet my sister?"

"Yes. She came to our office with Mr. Feingold shortly after he hired us. She gave us a lot of information. I don't think she murdered her husband, just so you know."

"I'm glad to hear it. I know she and Gary were having some issues, but he was a good guy and I know they loved each other."

"Please let everyone know we are sorry for what happened and she is in our thoughts."

"Thank you. I'll tell them."

We said goodbye and left. Tina was quiet on our walk to the car and she remained so on the drive home.

After pulling in the drive and shutting the engine off, she remained in the car.

"Harry, you and Bea aren't going anywhere. Are you?"

"I don't think so, why?"

"I mean, you aren't leaving. Moving out. Are you?"

"No. No, Sis, we're not moving out."

"Thank you."

"You're welcome. We love you. We're not going anywhere."

Then she leaned over and kissed my cheek.

20

YAKUZA

Thursday Morning, 13 February

SNOW FELL DURING THE NIGHT. ENOUGH SO I HAD TO GO OUT AND shovel the doggone sidewalk when I let Buddy out before making breakfast.

When we entered the office, after disposing of soft boiled eggs, bacon, and toast, we were looking at a temperature of twenty-eight and a windchill of eighteen. All of us were drinking hot tea. Tina and I were at our respective desks and Bea was on the chesterfield with her tatting.

Tina was clearly preoccupied. She was staring off into space. Her tea was probably growing cold because she didn't appear to be touching it. Suddenly, she snapped back to this dimension.

"Harry, get a pad of paper. Let's go over our suspects."

I got out a legal pad and a pen.

"Let's start with Barlow's murder. Number one on the police list is Celeste. She had the means and possibly the opportunity. What about motive?"

I was writing on paper. "As I see it, possibly elimination. Get him out of the way because she'd fallen in love with someone else.

Or gain. Get his money. Otherwise, I don't really see any other motive."

"That's how I see it, too. However, she's running a business in which she cuckold's her husband every day. If she fell in love with someone, why not simply divorce him? No, I see no need to eliminate him. As for gain, she is wealthy herself and pulling in around a million a year. That's a lot of cash. I just don't see gain as a motive either. Therefore, as far as I'm concerned, I think Celeste is off the hook."

I jotted notes on the paper.

"Now, what about Barlow's sister. What was her name?"

I paged through a file on my desk. "Tracy Lee Barlow. Thirty-seven. No kids. Divorced three times because she likes to occupy other men's beds. She should really join the polyamory community. Anyway, I don't see that she stands to gain anything from her brother's death."

"Neither do I. So what about Celeste's siblings?"

"There's her brother, Bridger."

Tina looked at the ceiling and closed her eyes. "No opportunity and I don't see any motive. The guy is richer than Donald Trump. No, nothing there."

I wrote on the pad of paper.

"So that leaves Nicole." Tina lowered her head and opened her eyes. "Why would she want to get rid of her brother-in-law?"

"I can't think of a single reason. Her brother, maybe. But not the late Gary Barlow."

"Same here. She wouldn't gain anything. I don't see any need to eliminate him and I can't imagine jealousy being an issue, nor revenge. No, there doesn't seem to be anything there."

"So then, Boss, the families are out."

"That's what I think. What about the church people?"

"They're a sad lot."

Tina chuckled. "I agree. And if any of them were a strong possibility, the police would be on them like white on rice."

"True." I jotted notes on paper.

"So I think we can eliminate the Vander Walles and Emily Stevens. Even though Phebe and James are out, they have sufficiently large egos to qualify."

"I don't think either could stand to get their hands icky with blood and guts."

Tina laughed and mouthed the word, *no*.

I scratched my head. "So who does that leave us with?"

"The Japanese man who left his card for Reverend Gary Barlow."

"We know nothing about him."

"No, we don't. He is, however, the only suspect we have left."

I put the pen down. "What motive?"

"What motive, indeed? My guess? Something to do with the time Barlow was in San Francisco."

"What makes you say that?"

"Two things, Harry. First, I did more research on seppuku. The internet is a wonderful tool. I found instructions on how to perform the four possible cuts for committing ritual suicide. The one done to Reverend Barlow was one of the four cuts."

My eyebrows went up. "So the person wasn't just making a statement."

"No. He, or she, knew exactly what he or she was doing and simply chose a cut which offered a graphic pun as well as an efficient means of dispatching the victim."

"Okay, what's number two?"

She leaned back in her chair and put her hands behind her head. "Ever hear of the Yakuza?"

"No."

Bea spoke without looking up from her tatting. "Aren't they like the Mafia?"

Tina brought her chair back to normal and raised her eyebrows. "Why, yes, Bea, they are. How do you know about them?"

"Some program on TV." Bea stopped tatting and looked up at

the ceiling. "PBS, I think. Maybe two or three years ago." She went back to work on her lace.

"Reason number two is the Yakuza. When I was in San Francisco my partner in the art gallery and I had to deal with them. One of the families, the Akiyama-ikka, had moved in from Japan. They were expanding their reach. We had to pay them protection money. Not a lot, but enough. We worked out a deal. Every month we gave them paintings worth a thousand dollars and they left us alone. The family head for San Francisco liked art. It was a sweet deal."

Bea asked, "Didn't that hurt your inventory?"

"In a way." Tina put her hands behind her head. "They didn't get originals. They got fakes."

Bea's face showed surprise. "Oh."

Tina went on. "As I recall, over the year we had to pay, I passed to them quite a number of original works of art, my original works. I created seven paintings in the style of H. R. Fish. Fish was a minor northern California woman artist. I couldn't even find a complete catalog of her work. So I faked her style and her signature and the paintings took care of two month's protection. Even today, her work doesn't go for much. I figured who'd bother to check?"

"But, Tina, what if they'd found out?" Concern was heavy in Bea's voice.

"Then we would have been in a lot of trouble. But we didn't have a thousand bucks lying around just to give to a gang of criminals. I also faked the work of Charles S. Graham, Granville Redmond and Henry Percy Gray. The last two are well-known artists. We had to go to some lengths on those two. We concocted stories and faked authentication certificates. We stuck it to old Kazuo Akiyama. He thought he was getting some valuable art for a song. What he got were fakes worth essentially nothing."

I let out a whistle.

Bea was shaking her head. "Wow. They were bad and you were bad."

"Perhaps I was. But they were people doing a whole lot of bad things all the time. Probably still are. I actually liked Mr. Akiyama. He was a nice old man. But he got his money through extortion, pimping, drugs, and lord knows what else. The Akiyama-ikka wasn't and probably still isn't a nice organization."

"I guess not," Bea said. "There's sure a lot of icky stuff going on in the world."

I laughed. "That there is, Babe." I turned to Tina. "You know I saw at the Barlow house a Fish painting and two Grahams I know you've copied. Only these didn't have your signature on them."

"Really? Hm. Wonder if old Mr. Akiyama discovered they were fakes after all?"

"Maybe. So, what about the Japanese fellow?"

"I think he's with the Yakuza and Barlow ran afoul of them in San Francisco."

"So this is a revenge killing?" I asked.

"Probably."

I leaned back in my chair.

Tina said, "The question is how to find this guy."

I leaned forward. "Should *we* find him? After all, we're on hold. If the police had this, they might be able to run him to ground."

Tina leaned back in her chair and closed her eyes. I took note of the clock on my desk and the time it was telling me. One minute. Two minutes. Three minutes. This was a major struggle. She didn't want to let go. I suppose she felt personally invested due to her past. Bea looked at me. I shrugged. Four minutes.

She sat up. Four minutes and twenty-seven seconds. "Give it to Cal."

"Consider it done." And I picked up my desk phone.

21

WHO GETS THE BARLOW MILLIONS?

Thursday Afternoon, 13 February

MY PHONE CALL TO CAL DIDN'T GO WELL. I THOUGHT HE'D BE HAPPY as a dog with a brand new bone. He wasn't.

"So. The Red Baron's been holding out on us again."

"No, Cal. Honest. We just came to this conclusion ourselves."

"No offense, Harry. Maybe *you* just came to this conclusion, but my next paycheck says the Red Baron knew about this Yaku-whatever a long time ago. She's been sitting on this waiting for the right opportunity so it makes a big splash and makes her look indispensable. I know how she works. She grandstands. It's going to cost her one day. Going to cost her her license. Thanks for the info."

I was left with a dial tone in my ear. No goodbye. At least he said "thanks". Wonder what's eating him? I relayed the information to Tina. She, too, looked surprised and then shrugged. Bea, too, was taken aback.

After disposing of a goodly quantity of leftovers for lunch, we returned to the office. Bea's attention was diverted by a couple of phone calls, which left Tina and I looking at each other from our respective desks.

I decided to break the ice. "Are we going to do anything about Celeste?"

"You mean as in tracking down the person who shot her?"

I nodded.

"We have no client."

"We could chase the ambulance, as it were."

"We could. Which would put us right in Cal's sights."

"True. So we are just going to sit here?"

"We have no client and after his comment to you…" She shrugged.

"So we are just going to sit here."

"I was going to consider suspects, but not now. If we are hired to investigate some aspect of her attempted murder, then we'll investigate."

"I see. Okay. You're the boss."

Bea came bouncing in. "There are two appointments tomorrow. J. Allen McGuire at ten and Cathy Able at three. McGuire is looking for industrial counter-espionage help and Able wants us to track her ex-husband."

"Thank you, Bea," Tina said.

"You're welcome!" And she bounced back out to her desk.

Tina pushed back her chair. "You can deal with the Able appointment. I'm not interested. I'll be in the music room." She stood and left the office.

I walked out to Bea's desk and with a movement of my head indicated she should join me in the Inner Sanctum. She stood, walked around her desk, and walked with me over to the fireplace.

Bea whispered, "Why the secrecy?"

I didn't whisper. I did, however, keep my voice low. "Do you get the feeling something's up with Tina?"

"Kind of. Kind of like she's not all here."

"There's that. Remember what she said this morning? 'Let's start with Barlow's murder'?"

Bea nodded.

"She didn't go anywhere after that. I was expecting we'd start looking at motive for the attack on Celeste. The phone call to Cal put the kibosh on that, or so it seems to me. Tina's never let running afoul of Cal dictate what she does or doesn't do."

"Boy, Harry, that is really interesting. Was Cal really pissed?"

"Yes, he was. I don't ever recall him threatening her license, though. That's new."

"Wow."

"Wow, indeed. Something is escalating something somewhere."

Bea giggled. "That was pretty definite, Mr. Wright."

I chuckled. "It was, wasn't it?" I winked at her. "What I meant was something is really pushing Cal's buttons and getting him riled up."

"Do you think Cal's found someone else?"

"Wouldn't be the first time. Although it's always been on their off times."

"Oh, boy. This isn't good."

"No, Babe. I don't think it is."

The phone rang and Bea left to get it.

I looked at the fire. Somebody killed Gary Barlow. Somebody tried to kill Celeste Barlow. Were those two acts related? That's a great big unknown. If they were, and if Tina's right, then the Yakuza is also after Celeste. But why? That, too, is a big unknown at this point.

If they aren't then the question begs to be asked, will the shooter make another attempt on Celeste? Of course, it is possible and most likely probable. And if he or she is successful, are the children in danger? If the kids died, who'd get the Barlow millions?

22

RIDICULOUS

Thursday Night, 13 February

IT DIDN'T TAKE LONG TO FIND OUT WHO WOULD INHERIT IF THE Barlow children died with no will. A very quick search revealed probate would probably give the money to their grandparents. Mrs. Collins didn't need the money and, from the sounds of it, neither did Mr. and Mrs. Barlow. No motive for murder there that I could see. I bounced my conclusion off Tina and she agreed.

We were sitting in the living room by the fire. Supper eaten, we were having after dinner drinks. I brought up the Yakuza. Tina frowned but indicated I should continue.

"What I don't get is this: if the Japanese fellow is a Yakuza member, why wait all this time to kill Barlow. We're talking some twenty-five years ago. That's a long time to wait to kill someone."

Tina took a sip of Malmsey. "It is. The Yakuza, like the Mafia, like an elephant, never forgets."

"Why not kill him back then?"

"Valid question. I don't know. I put in a call to my friend, Jeff Maybury, at the CIA. Hopefully, he can tell me something. If not, I may have to go out to San Francisco myself."

"And do what?" I asked.

"Find out why."

"Shouldn't we be turning this over to the police?" Bea asked.

"Maybe." Tina was clearly not interested in pursuing the conversation.

"You're not going to, though," I said.

"Not yet."

"And why would someone shoot Celeste?"

"I don't know, Harry. We need Celeste's will."

"Shouldn't we ask Feingold about that?"

"We're on hold *and* we aren't investigating Celeste's shooting."

"What's with you?" I demanded. "You aren't yourself."

"I don't want to upset Cal."

"His feelings never mattered before."

"They do now. I want him to come back to me."

Well, there it was. In the open. She was letting her love for Cal dictate our business practice. There was nothing more for me to say. And I didn't.

Tina finished her wine and excused yourself. "I'll be in my room. Good night you two."

We wished her a good night and she left.

"There it is, Harry. She really wants Cal back."

"And this time I have a feeling it's going to bite her in the ass."

"I hope not."

"Me, too, Babe. Me too. In the meantime, I think we need to get the ball rolling on this. Feingold's sitting on his butt and Tina's sitting on her butt. And the cops? Who knows where the hell they're at. I can tell you one thing: even with us giving them the possible Yakuza connection, they aren't going to know what to do with it. Then there's Celeste. We're holding the key to that one, too. At least I'm guessing we are. Tina could wrap up a murder and an attempted murder and all of a sudden she doesn't want to hurt Cal's feelings."

All I could do was shake my head. It all sounded so ridiculous.

23

THE QUEEN AWAKES

Friday Morning, 14 February

BEA NUDGED ME. "HARRY. YOUR PHONE IS RINGING."

I patted around on the nightstand, more from rote than from a conscious effort to find the thing, found it, and answered the call.

"Sorry to wake you, Harry. I'm in the hospital. Regions."

"Wait. I'm still sleeping. David?"

"Sorry. Yes, David Nagasawa. I got mugged, Harry. I'm at Regions Hospital. I have a broken leg. Not bad. But broken nonetheless. The muggers gave me a message to pass on. They said, 'Leave Barlow alone. Justice has been served.' Do you know what it means?"

I was fully awake. "David, did you see your attackers?"

"The light wasn't good. They jumped me. I fought back. I think I busted a nose and maybe an arm. There were too many of them and they finally pinned me down, punched me a couple times, and held me. They gave me the message and stomped my leg. Asian. They were Asian, and I'm thinking Japanese. There aren't many of us in the Cities, so we kind of stand out."

"Thanks for the info and sorry about your leg. When are you going home?"

"I'm free to go now."

"You have a ride?"

"Not yet."

"Hang tight. I'll take you home."

"You sure?"

"Of course, I'm sure. Give me half an hour."

"Thanks, Harry."

"Don't mention it."

We disconnected and I got out of bed.

"What is it, Harry?"

"I think our Japanese suspect has friends. Somebody beat up David and broke his leg. He's at Regions Hospital. I'm going to take him home. Tell Tina, if you see her before I do, David was roughed up by some fellows who he thinks were Japanese. They broke his leg and said to him: 'Leave Barlow alone. Justice has been served.'"

"Wow. These Barlows are attracting a lot of bad karma. And now anyone connected with them."

"Looks that way, doesn't it?"

I threw on some clothes, kissed Bea goodbye, grabbed the keys for the Flex, and drove over to St Paul and the hospital. David was there, waiting. He hobbled out to the car on his crutches. Once he was in, I headed for his place.

"Sorry about your leg, David. You have insurance?"

"I do. Don't worry about it, Harry. Occupational hazard."

"That it is."

"Any idea what the second part of the message means?"

"I'm not sure. Tina passed our information on the Japanese fellow to Cal. She suspects Barlow ran afoul of the Yakuza in San Francisco and thinks Barlow's death might be a Yakuza revenge killing."

"That's not good. They're bad, Harry."

"So I'm discovering."

"But that makes the message understandable. I think Tina's on the money."

"So it would seem."

"Which means, if they came after me, Lois, at the church, could be in danger."

"Crap. Hadn't thought of that. Better let Cal know."

"It also means, they have eyes and ears around."

"It does. Doesn't it?" I fished my phone out of my pocket and gave it to David. He turned it on and I told it to call 'Cal'. He answered on the fifth ring.

"Swenson."

"Cal. Harry Wright here. David Nagasawa was attacked several hours ago by —," I looked at David and he held up four and then five fingers, "—by four or five guys. They broke his leg and told him to, and I quote, 'Leave Barlow alone. Justice has been served.' David thinks Lois Gorman, at the church Barlow pastored, might be in danger."

"Thanks, Harry. I'll see to it we have some men at her place."

"Thanks, Cal."

"Anything else?"

"Not at the moment."

"Tell David I hope his leg heals quickly."

"I'll do that."

"Bye." And he disconnected.

"Do you think, David, there's anything Tina needs to know?"

"I don't know much. I just know they play rough. Very rough."

"We'll keep our eyes and ears open."

When we got to David's place, I helped him get settled and then I drove back to Tina's palace. With the car safely parked in the garage, I unlocked the back door, and entered the house. I smelled something cooking and made my way to the kitchen. There was Bea making buckwheat pancakes.

"There's my man." Spatula in hand, Bea came up to me and I took her in my arms and kissed her. "How's David?" she asked.

"He's doing okay, considering. They could have really messed him up and didn't."

"Lucky him." She moved back over to the stove and flipped pancakes.

"Indeed."

"Does he have somebody?"

"He lives alone. That I know for sure. Although I believe he does have a pooky who hangs out with him a lot. He doesn't say much about her. She's a bonsai person."

"Friends with benefits?"

"Probably."

Bea removed the pancake and added it to the stack on the plate. While she poured more batter, I buttered the hot cake.

Tina poked her head into the kitchen. "Bea's making breakfast? Is this a new routine?"

"No, Sis. David got mugged by our Yakuza friends." I told her about David's phone call and me taking him home.

She stroked her chin. "It seems they're here in the Cities and that Barlow's past caught up with him."

"Seems that way," I said.

Bea asked, while removing another pancake from the griddle, "Is there any way to break them up before they get too established?"

"Hanging the murder on them will help," Tina replied, "providing they aren't already established."

"And that is assuming the police can find our suspect," I added.

"True. And unfortunately, the Yakuza is very careful," Tina said.

Pancakes cooked, we adjourned to the dining room and ate our breakfast. Discussing the eruption of Mount Kelud in Java and Maduro arresting opposition activists. Afterwards, we went to the office. From one of my desk drawers, I took out Valentine's Day gifts of chocolate for my two favorite girls. Tina gave me a gift certificate to my favorite tea shop and Bea gave me a bottle of absinthe, a different brand of the liqueur than the one Tina gave me at Christmas so I could make comparisons.

Not quite quarter to ten, the phone rang. A minute later Bea poked her head in and said the call was from Feingold. Celeste was awake. I thought it appropriate for Sunny Day, queen of the online empire of love, to awake on Valentine's Day.

Tina turned from looking at the computer screen. "Are we back on the job?"

"He didn't say."

"Call him back and ask him."

"Okay." Bea disappeared back into the outer office. She reappeared shortly and said we were back on the case.

Tina closed her eyes and stroked her chin. When she opened them she picked up a pad of paper and a pencil and started writing.

The doorbell rang and a perturbed look flitted across her face. In a moment Bea ushered in a thirty-ish looking fellow wearing blue jeans, a plaid flannel shirt, and a brown corduroy sport coat. Bea informed us his name was J. Allen McGuire.

I introduced Tina and myself and guided him to the oxblood oversize wingback. McGuire was tall and lanky. He needed a bit more girth to look good in that chair.

Tina came straight to the point. "What can we help you with Mr McGuire?"

"Someone's spying on my company and passing on secrets to my competitor."

"Who's your competitor?"

"Rahman Software."

"What secrets are they passing on?"

"Seems like everything. I mean Rahman knows my appointments, memos, email."

"How big is your company?"

"I have fifteen employees. I lost a big contract because Rahman somehow learned my bid and made a lower one."

"When was this?"

"Two months ago."

'When did you first become aware of this problem?"

"That's what tipped me off. Someone must have given that information to Rahman."

"Who knew about the bid?"

"Just myself and Jane Norgard, who handles contracts."

"Why isn't Jane the mole?"

"Because information she wouldn't have access to has gone over to Rahman as well."

"Who runs Rahman Software?"

"Abu Muhammad Nazari."

"Have you ever met him?"

"Yes. At a conference. Three, four months ago. Seemed like an okay guy. Friendly. His wife was reserved around me, but got on okay with Alison."

"Alison is…?"

"Oh, sorry. My wife."

"How was your wife with Nazari?"

"Friendly."

"How's your marriage, Mr. McGuire?"

"My marriage? Why do you ask? What does that have to do with this?"

"I don't know. Might be pertinent."

"I see. I guess, it's okay."

"You guess?"

"Been a bit rocky lately. I've been putting in long hours trying to do damage control."

Tina pursed her lips. "Do you always take your laptop with you?"

"Oh, yes. It's really my office."

"Do you have five hundred dollars?"

"Not on me."

"A credit card?"

"Yes."

"Give Mr. Wright your credit card. Harry, charge Mr McGuire five hundred dollars."

"Wait a minute. What's this about?"

"Do you want to know who the mole is?"

"Yes."

"It will cost you five hundred dollars. If I'm wrong, you'll get your money back."

"Okay." He fished his credit card out of his wallet and handed it to me. I made the charge, gave him back the card, and emailed the receipt to him for five hundred dollars."

"Let me see your laptop."

McGuire handed it to her. "It's password protected."

"Unlock it, please." She pushed the computer back towards our client.

McGuire got up, unlocked it, and passed it back to her.

Tina tapped on keys and moved her finger on the track pad for ten minutes or so and then asked, "Who has access to this?"

"No one. Just me."

"Where do you hide your passwords?"

"They're all on the computer. Autofill."

"What about the master password to unlock the laptop?"

"Oh, that one I have in my wallet."

"Someone installed a keylogger on your computer. My guess is your wife did so because she is seeing Mr. Nazari and he asked her to."

"What? How…?" He just sat there with his mouth open.

"Remove the keylogger, change all your passwords, and find a more secure hiding place for your master password."

"But what about my wife? Why would you say something like that?"

"Because she's the most likely suspect. She'd have access to your wallet. An affair with Nazari is the most likely reason she'd have for betraying you. But you can ask her or him about all that."

McGuire was clearly shell shocked. I got up, retrieved his computer for him, and guided him to the outer office, where Bea took over.

Back at my desk, I said, "Don't you think you could have sugarcoated it?"

"I suppose. Honestly. He's a computer guy. And he doesn't even know a keylogger has been installed on his laptop?" She shook her head. "Besides, we have a murder and an attempted murder to investigate."

It was my turn and I shook my head. Sometimes my sister can be pretty doggone cold.

She picked up her pencil and pulled the pad of paper so it was back in front of her. "Now, Harry, what is hindering our progress is lack of motive. Do you agree?"

I told her I did.

"I think it likely Gary Barlow's death was due to a Yakuza hit. But why? Even if we say revenge, the question begs to be asked, revenge for what? What did he do that got their ire up? And what was the reason for someone trying to kill Celeste? What the police don't know but we do is that two people stand to gain from her demise: Nussbaum and sister Nicole. There might be other people with other motives, however those two are at present known to us and we'll have to run with them until the evidence shows they didn't try to kill her."

Suddenly it hit me. Tina was talking about the attempt on Celeste's life. We weren't going to pursue it and now we were. I said nothing. No sense in spoiling things by questioning her. "So the murder and attempted murder are not related."

"Unknown. It's possible we are missing some connection. However, with our current information it seems unlikely."

"Do we still want her will?"

"I think so. If nothing else, it gives us more data."

I picked up the phone, dialed, and, when Lolana answered, asked her if Feingold had done Celeste's will. She checked the computer and told me he hadn't and they didn't have a copy. I thanked her, hung up, and relayed the information to Tina.

She looked up from the notepad. "If there was one at the house, the police probably have it. Call Mrs. Collins and see if she might have a copy."

I called and spoke with Genevieve. She said she'd call me back.

"Harry, let's pay Celeste a visit."

"Your car or mine?"

She gave me a puzzled look. The reason being due to us always taking her car. She prefers to drive and in fact almost always does.

"Just being polite," I said.

She rolled her eyes.

24

NO VISIT

Friday Afternoon, 14 February

HENNEPIN COUNTY MEDICAL CENTER IS A MASSIVE PLACE ON THE east side of the downtown district in Minneapolis. Today, for some reason, parking was difficult to find. Tina ended up at a meter four blocks away. Ramp, lot, or street, they all cost and they all cost a lot. If the city could figure out a way to charge for the air we breathe, they'd probably do it.

In my opinion, big cities are expensive. All that infrastructure to maintain. And they tax you accordingly. An additional downside is basic shopping, such as for groceries, is much more difficult to find and much more expensive than in the 'burbs. Especially taxable items, because the city tax on top of the state tax is outrageous. Tina, though, likes living in the city and so there we are.

The sky was clear and, in the winter, that means a cold day in Minnesota. Today was no exception. Fourteen above zero and a windchill of one above. We were plenty bundled up and I still felt as though someone had put ice cubes in my gloves and shoes. The weather in Minnesota sucks. Plain and simple.

We made it to the hospital, inquired if Celeste Barlow had been moved, were told she had, and got her new room number. We took the elevator to her floor and found her room, only to be stopped by the police guard. We didn't have access and he wasn't anyone we knew who might be willing to fudge for us.

Tina scowled. "Does Harold Feingold have access?" she demanded.

The cop looked at us and sounded bored when he spoke. "Yes."

"We work for him."

"Is your name 'Harold Feingold'?"

"No."

"His?" The cop nodded his head in my direction.

"No."

"Then you aren't allowed in."

Now Tina was really pissed. I know, because *she* called Feingold's office.

"Lolana, this is Justinia Wright. Is Mr. Feingold in? No? Very well. Tell him we need to be put on the list to see Celeste Barlow." There was a pause and then, "Thank you."

Tina put her phone in her purse, said, "Come on, Harry, might as well go home," and started walking. At the elevator we met the Collins and Barlow families. I introduced Tina to Mrs. Collins and she in turn introduced us to her son, Bridger, his wife Stacy, Nicole, who we had met on our previous visit to the hospital, to Gary's parents, Carlton and Dotty, and Gary's sister, Tracy Lee.

Mrs. Collins asked how Celeste was and I told her we weren't on the list of approved visitors and couldn't see her.

"Oh, what nonsense. Come with us." Mrs. Collins is quite spunky.

Tina smiled, "Thank you, but the guard has his orders. We have a call in to Mr. Feingold to correct the situation. You can, though, help us."

"How so?" Mrs. Collins asked.

"Do you have a copy of Celeste's will?"

"I believe so. Call Genevieve. She'll know for sure."

Nicole volunteered, "If Mom doesn't have one, I do."

Tina thanked them, said how pleased we were to meet everyone, and then entered an elevator going down. I followed.

"Call Genevieve and have her fax it to us."

My phone was already in my hand. I waggled it in front of her and made the call. Genevieve said she'd found the will and we should get it within the hour. I thanked her and relayed the info to Tina.

"What do you think of them?" she asked.

"Mrs. Collins is a nice lady. Bridger has pompous ass written all over his face. His wife could be Mrs. Pompous Ass. Nicole is just too plain to be a hooker, in my opinion. Especially a high class one. Maybe she uses a lot of makeup. Carlton and Dotty have the typical old money smell. Now Tracy Lee, *she* could be a hooker.

"Yes. I saw her eyes linger on your crotch."

"They did?"

"Yes. Where were you looking?"

"Obviously not at her."

"Then how do you know she could be a hooker?"

"Good grief."

Tina chuckled and had a big grin plastered on her face.

25

PRIME SUSPECTS

Friday Night, 14 February

TINA STUCK ME WITH SEEING CATHY ABLE AT 3 PM BECAUSE SHE hates missing person cases and Ms. Able wanted us to find her missing ex-husband. As it turned out, Ms. Able called in two hours before her appointment and told Bea she couldn't make it.

That left the afternoon free to ruminate on the case and decide the best course of action.

Unfortunately, I was pretty much at sea and Tina was playing a string of Amy Beach piano pieces. So I contented myself with a look through of Celeste's will, a copy of which Genevieve had faxed to us earlier in the afternoon. The copy I'd made for Tina was on her desk. She might get to it after her frolic with Beach.

And since we had to eat, I decided to make something hearty to warm the spirits on this chilly night. Flipping through my recipes, Bangers and Mash jumped out at me and because there were a few excellent sausages from Kramarczuk's in the fridge I went ahead and indulged my British taste buds.

After supper, we retired to the office. Bea brought her tatting and we all sat by the fire. Tina and I read through the will looking to see who if anyone got what.

To my eyes, even on the second go through, the document looked to contain nothing but standard legal mumbo jumbo. I paid the most attention to the part outlining what happens should Celeste predecease her husband and if he should predecease her or they leave this sunny vale at the same time. And even all that was pretty much standard. If the children were minors, the money would go into a trust for them. If adults, they each got half the estate.

When I finished, Tina said, "Well?"

"I didn't see anything out of the ordinary. Did you?"

"No. What is of significance is there is no provision for the money should the children die without heirs. You've already pointed out that according to state law the probate court would probably give the money to the grandparents, should they be alive."

"And we concluded the grandparents wouldn't need the money and so are off the hook for trying to off Celeste."

"Correct." Tina took a sip of madeira and puffed on her cigar. "So unless someone intends to wipe out the family, I don't think the children are in danger."

"Makes sense."

"However, she might have been shot for her money from the bordello empire, which is not in the will."

"True. Which means our primary suspects are Nussbaum and Nicole."

"Correct again, Harry."

"What are you going to do?"

"I think we need to track Nicole's and Nussbaum's movements. We need to know what they are up to."

What was this she was saying? She really was going to pursue Celeste's shooting without us getting a client. "Wait. Hold your horses. You said we weren't going to get involved with Celeste's shooting because we didn't have a client and you didn't want to upset Cal. What happened to change your mind?"

"Harry, sometimes... Look, Feingold wants us to get Celeste

off the hook. We either find who killed Gary Barlow, and I think we have, our mysterious Japanese fellow, or we give Celeste an alibi, which we have in our possession. Namely, she was meeting with Nussbaum."

"So let's give the info to the police and be done with it."

"We could. Someone, however, tried to kill Celeste. Why now? The murder of Gary and the attempted murder of Celeste are coincidental? Occurring so close together? I find that unlikely. The more I think about it the more I'm thinking something connects the two. The question is what? What makes sense or even what doesn't make sense but works?"

Bea, not looking up from her tatting, said, "It could be they share the same person but not the same motive."

Tina and I stared at Bea.

She looked up. "What?"

"That's very astute of you, Bea," Tina said.

A big smile broke out on my honey's face. "Thanks!"

Tina cocked her head to one side and looked at the ceiling. "Which means, the Yakuza had a hand in both."

"Or Nussbaum had a hand in both," I added.

"Or," and a smile appeared on Tina's face, "the Yakuza *and* Nussbaum are involved in both."

"What about the police?" Bea asked. "They don't know about Nussbaum or Nicole."

"No, they don't," Tina said. "I guess their search for evidence wasn't as creative as Harry's."

"So shouldn't we give this to Cal?" Bea asked. "That way they will have all the information."

"We could give what we have to him and hopefully they would make all the right conclusions. However, why give him a little fish when we can give him a great big one?"

Tina is always looking for a chance to grandstand. In that, Cal is right. I said, "I think we should give him the info and call it a day."

"We're going to get more evidence and then give it to Cal. A great big present."

I shrugged. "Okay. You're the boss."

Bea looked up from her tatting. "I hope you don't get in trouble, Tina."

"Thanks, for your concern, Bea. It will be all right." She looked at me. "Before we start tracking Nussbaum and Nicole, Harry, we should talk to them again."

"Okay. I'll call them tomorrow."

We passed another hour of idle chitchat and then Tina excused herself and went to bed. When she was gone, Bea brought up the subject of Cal.

"He didn't give her a Valentine's Day gift."

"No, he didn't. It's happened before."

"But if he's thinking of moving back here, doesn't it make sense for him to get her a gift?"

"One would think so. Maybe because of the case he didn't want to bring it over. The conflict of interest thing."

"Yeah, but if he loved her he'd have found a way to get her a gift without being flashy about it. Do you think he's changed his mind?"

"Possible."

"Oh, dear. She'll be devastated."

"Probably."

"I was so hoping."

"I know. They're a pair of modern star-crossed lovers, that's for sure."

"Do you think she suspects?"

"Yes, I think she suspects. This isn't anything new, really."

"Oh."

"Probably why she wants to give him a big present with the case. Butter him up. Even let him take the credit."

"I see."

"Hopefully, when the case is over everything will have worked out so they can be happily together forever and a day."

"I hope so." I could tell by Bea's tone of voice she was beginning to think there wasn't a lot to be hoped for.

There was a long pause, which Bea finally broke. "I'm very sad, Harry. Will you make love to me and promise me you'll never leave me?"

I stood, took her hand, and we went upstairs to our bedroom. You can take it from there.

26

NICOLE

Saturday, 15 February

The morning routine was nothing out of the ordinary. Let Buddy out, shower, get dressed, avoid dog chasing cats or cats chasing dog, make tea, prepare breakfast, serve breakfast, read the paper, and then clean up the dishes. Since we had a case, today was a work day and I had phone calls to make.

The first one was to Nussbaum. He was very reluctant to meet with us, but agreed to do so tomorrow at eleven. The second call was to Nicole and since she was staying at her mother's I was also able to find out from Genevieve that Barlow's funeral was to be held tomorrow at two. Nicole said she could meet with us today at one. I relayed the information to Tina, who was sitting at her desk and staring off into space.

"Thanks, Harry." She reached towards the humidor and her cell phone started playing Glass's "Metamorphosis II". That's her incoming call ringtone. She took a look at the phone. "I need to take this in private, Big Brother."

I saluted and left. Bea usually doesn't work in the office on the weekends. She does the grocery shopping and cleaning mostly then. If we're not on a case, I help her. She was vacuuming upstairs, which meant my occupying the library was probably safe from interruption and so I occupied it. I picked up *The Unconsoled* by Kazuo Ishiguro and began reading.

After some time passed, not sure how much as I didn't check my watch, I was summoned to the office. *The Unconsoled* would have to wait. I put the book down and made my way to the command center.

"I'm going out tonight and possibly again tomorrow night. Ask me no questions and I'll tell you no lies."

I hadn't even gotten to my desk when my sister blurted that one out. My response was a simple, "Okay." I continued on to my desk and sat in my chair.

What she was telling me, I think, was she got information about something to do with our case and was not going to tell me what it was for my own good. Most likely because her response to said information was going to be something not within the bounds of what was considered legally permissible. Sometimes I wonder if Tina is still working for the CIA and just not telling us about it.

Since it would be helpful to know, I asked, "Will you be coming home after your adventure?"

"Probably."

"Okay. How are you going to approach Nicole?"

"Not sure. I'll decide that when I see her."

Since there was some time to kill before Sunny Day, Junior showed up, I went out to the kitchen and started working on lunch and supper. Because we'd have to be back in the office by one, I decided on sandwiches for lunch. To satisfy Tina's meat tooth, for supper I decided to have steak smothered in mushroom sauce, with baked potato rebaked with cheese and broccoli, and a tossed salad. That should keep her satisfied while she's on her mysterious mission.

When noon rolled around, I called the ladies to lunch. Bea's been thinking of selling the house she bought after she sold her late spouse's pile and buying something where we might want to retire. We discussed the pros and cons over our sandwiches and chenin blanc. Having disposed of the sandwiches and wine, Tina and I left Bea to clean up and returned to the office. We'd just gotten settled when the doorbell started ringing. I went to the door, took a look through the peephole, saw Nicole, and opened the door.

"Right on time, Ms. Collins. Come in."

She entered and I took her coat, hanging it on a peg in the entryway. I guided her into the inner office and to the oxblood wingback. Because introductions had already been performed, I didn't bother, and settled in at my desk to take notes.

"How is your sister?" Tina asked, arms folded on her desk.

"She's improving."

"Any idea who might want to see her dead?"

"No."

"Certainly not you."

"Of course not! She's my sister."

"That is no argument in your favor. Sisters have killed sisters many times over in the past millennia. And with Celeste out of the way, you become Sunny Day. Plenty of motive, if you ask me."

"Well, I'm not asking."

"Then again, there's your boyfriend. Get rid of Celeste, get rid of you, and he has the whole empire to himself."

"Are you talking about Flinny?"

"Flinders Nussbaum, yes."

"He's not my boyfriend and he already gets paid a lot of money."

"So I hear. But there's nothing like having the whole enchilada, so to speak."

"You have a sick mind."

"You're not the first person to say so. Those who do usually have something to hide or are guilty."

"Well, I'm neither."

"Actually, you have a lot to hide, Ms. Collins."

Nicole said nothing and Tina pushed her chair away from her

desk, leaned back, and crossed her legs. "What's it like being Celeste's sister?"

"You know, I think I've had enough." Nicole stood.

"Harry, call Lieutenant Swenson and tell him we have a present for him."

Nicole sat.

"You'll answer my question?"

"What do you think it's like?"

"I've only had him—," Tina pointed to me, "—to live with. To hazard a guess, I'd say difficult. She's beautiful, sexy, self-assured, in control, doesn't give a damn. You probably tried to get approval by being the good little girl. Am I right?"

"That's basically it."

"Sorry to hear you say so. Still—," Tina sat up, "—it doesn't excuse attempted murder."

"I didn't shoot her. I may not like her overly much, but I do love her. When I needed help, she was right there. Gave me money. A lot of money. Then offered me a partnership in her business. At first, I thought she was kidding. She assured me she wasn't and showed me how it works. I felt funny about the whole idea at first. I mean, being a hooker? Celeste, though, made it sound all fun and glamorous. She has this way about her, you know?"

Tina nodded.

"And in a way it is fun and glamorous. It's like acting. Although the first few times I wasn't sure I wanted to go through with having sex with a strange man. Celeste though was there and helped me get over my inhibitions and guilt. And when I did let go, and had some real mind-blowing sex... All I can say is wow. Being a high-class hooker isn't so bad. Wouldn't want to be on the street. But what I'm doing? It's pretty good. And then there is the money. And there is lots of money. Since we became adults, Celeste has been fair with me. I would never shoot her. Never."

"What about Nussbaum?"

"No. Flinny wouldn't do that. He has a good gig and he likes

Celeste a lot. Sometimes— Well, he likes her. I don't think he'd shoot her. What would his reason be?"

"Money."

"But he has money."

"More money."

She shook her head. "No. I don't think so."

"You love him."

She nodded.

"He love you?"

She shrugged. "I don't know. I think so. He likes Celeste and, well, he wouldn't be the first boyfriend I lost to her."

"I think we are done for now, Ms. Collins. Thank you for your time."

Tina stood and so did Nicole. I escorted the escort to the front door, helped her into her coat, bid her a good day, and turned her out into the cold cruel world.

Back in the office, I walked up to Tina's desk.

"Nussbaum?"

She nodded. "Probably."

"I'll type up the notes."

"If I'm not here tomorrow, talk to Nussbaum, and then give Cal everything."

I raised my eyebrows. "Everything?"

"Contingency plan, Harry."

Something serious was going down tonight. Something very serious.

27

FLYING GLASS

Saturday Night, 15 February

AFTER SUPPER, TINA LEFT. SHE WAS DRESSED IN A ONE PIECE BLACK bodysuit and black boots. The bodysuit also had a tight fitting hood. I didn't like the looks of it. I could only think she was going on the warpath.

When she was gone, Bea asked, "Where is she going?"

"I don't have the foggiest, Babe, and I don't think I really want to know."

What I didn't tell Bea is that Tina has a storage unit, a large garage, really. She keeps her 1969 Alfa Romeo Spider Veloce there. That much I know. Basically, the garage is off limits. So what else might be stored there is anybody's guess. Then, again, maybe nothing's stored there except over active imaginations.

The phone rang and Bea answered. After a minute, she hung up. "That was Harold Feingold. He said he finally got everything straightened out with the police. We should now be on the list to see Celeste. Apparently, there was some miscommunication and Nikki Nelson had taken us off the list."

"I don't believe that for a minute, Babe. Nikki is Cal's partner. I think she sabotaged the list. That or Cal told her to."

"Oh my God, Harry, that—"

A window exploded sending glass everywhere.

"Down!" I yelled.

More windows exploded in a shower of flying glass and there was the sound of gunshots.

"Harry! I'm bleeding. Bad."

I crawled over to Bea. Incurring cuts from glass along the way. Glass had cut her neck.

"This might hurt, Babe. I can't help it. Have to apply pressure to stop the bleeding."

I pressed on the wound to stop the flow of blood, or at least slow it down, with one hand and with the other, fished my cell phone out of my pocket and told it to call 911. When the operator answered, I gave her the address, described the injury, and described the attack.

"Hang in there, Babe. You're going to be all right. I love you."

On "I love you", she pointed to herself and then to me. Fear, though, danced in her eyes.

I kept pressing on her neck as hard as I dare. Forever is a long, long time and that's what it seemed was passing — forever. Paramedics and police finally arrived. Bea was rushed to the hospital. I called Melissa Olson at Three Sisters Security. Melissa and her twin sisters, Helen and Heloise, run a top-drawer security business. We've used their services in the past. I explained the situation and Melissa said she'd send Helen and Heloise over right away and would call an emergency service to board up the windows for us. I told her we owed her big time. Next, I explained to the police what happened and then surveyed the damage.

Almost every window on the ground floor had been shot out. Glass was everywhere and so were bullet holes. The temperature was around eighteen and the windchill was nine. The attack couldn't have lasted more than five minutes. When Helen and Heloise showed up, I vamoosed to the hospital to be with Bea.

The staff had admitted her for observation overnight. I went to her room and found her awake.

"Hi, Harry!"

"Hi, Babe. How are you doing?"

"They said I lost a lot of blood and gave me a transfusion. I should be able to go home tomorrow."

I kissed her.

"You saved my life."

"Of course. I love you and we haven't had enough time together."

"Thanks. You're the best thing that's ever happened to me."

I sat next to her and held her hand. With my other hand I touched her cheek. "Try to get some rest, my love."

"Okay. Are you going to stay with me?"

"I am."

She smiled and closed her eyes. Soon her breathing was soft and regular.

Someone was trying to scare us and maybe even kill us in the process. Tina doesn't scare. That much is certain. She's been through a lot and I don't even know a fourth of it. But from what she has intimated, working for Uncle Sam had some trying moments. Shooting up her house is going to make her very angry and she isn't a nice person when she's angry.

28

CONCERNED

Sunday Afternoon, 16 February

BEA AND I GOT HOME FROM THE HOSPITAL AT HALF-PAST ONE. TINA had made it back by eleven and Nussbaum was there, waiting. He was gone by the time we got home. So were Helen and Heloise. The repair crew had the place boarded up by seven this morning. The Twins left after explaining what they knew to Tina.

The three of us were in the office.

Tina spoke. "Nussbaum was very concerned about our safety and well-being. He was willing to reschedule. I wasn't. We went to the office and talked."

"What did you learn?" I asked.

"Very little." A big grin appeared on her face. "But perhaps enough. When I made a comment about the weather in San Francisco and our boarded up windows, he agreed. However, when I pursued it, he back pedaled and tried to blow it off. He didn't give us a very big doorway. It may, however, be all that we need."

"How so?"

"San Francisco seems to be the focal point. Gary Barlow was there under an assumed name for a year and came here. There is a Yakuza family there and they've opened a branch office here.

Nussbaum was apparently in Frisco and is now here. Too much of a coincidence if you ask me."

"Yet, it could be."

"Yes, Harry, it could be. Possible, but not probable in my book. The question in my mind is, were Barlow and Nussbaum acquainted with each other before? If not, then the Yakuza must be the connecting piece.

"Last night I learned that while only Japanese are trusted to be in leadership and in the higher circles of the organization, they make frequent use of non-Japanese in the lower levels and will even let the 'round eyes' join."

"Is that true?"

"It's as true, Harry, as the taking of a little finger can guarantee."

Bea made a noise and her hand flew to her mouth.

"This had to do with your adventure last night?"

"I don't know what you're talking about."

"Okay. Gotcha. All three were in San Fran and all three were here. That is a big coincidence."

"It is and now we need to find out why. When we do, we'll have solved the murder and gotten Celeste off the hook."

"And earned our pay."

"And earned our pay." She had a smug look on her face.

"So where do we start, O Great Detective?"

"We need to connect Nussbaum to the Yakuza. Gary Barlow's already connected, given how he died. Connect Flinders and we have our love triangle complete."

"How do we do that?"

"I'm not sure what the best path is to follow. This case has taken far too long already and we need to wrap it up."

"We could give it to Cal," Bea said.

"I love Cal, but the police will take forever to untangle this and in the meantime there could be more complications. We can end it and give them a nice tidy package with which their tidy bureaucratic minds can cope."

"Weren't you a bureaucrat?" I asked.

"Yes. If I would have thought like one I'd have ended up in a gulag or dead."

"So what's next?" I pressed.

"Let me think and while I do so, let's have lunch. You must be starved, Bea."

"Yeah. That hospital food is none too good."

Generally, we have plenty of leftovers and the fridge didn't disappoint. I brought out an array of containers and set up our own potluck. Each of us took what we wanted, nuked it, and went to the dining room. When we were all seated, Tina started talking.

"The Twins called a glass company. They'll be here sometime this afternoon to give us an estimate. Bea, I'd like you to handle the arrangements. Harry and I will be out."

Wow. The Boss *is* steamed. She never, and I mean never, gets this hands on in a case.

Tina continued, "I also want bulletproof glass installed. If they have it, I want transparent aluminum."

Bea giggled. "That's from *Star Trek*."

"It is and that's why the name's sometimes used for the new ceramics called transparent armor."

"Are you serious?" Bea's face showed surprise.

"I am."

"Wow. There's all kinds of stuff out there."

"There is, indeed, Bea," Tina said.

We finished lunch. Tina and I took the Flex and she had me drive. One, because she doesn't like the car for no other reason than it seats more than two. Secondly, she was going to be busy doing some snooping and didn't want to be bothered with driving. Our destination was Nussbaum's place out in Plymouth, a western suburb of Minneapolis. Not as spendy as Edina or Wayzata or North Oaks but there are some people with bucks living in Plymouth, including Mr. Nussbaum.

His house was in a nice quiet cul-de-sac by a park and a small lake. From the map, his backyard butts up to the lake.

"Don't go in the cul-de-sac, Harry. Park there at the corner so I have a view of his house."

I swung our behemoth around and parked it in the spot Tina wanted. She went to work setting up the data extraction device. We had his phone number. Now the task was to separate his phone from all the other cell phones and then strip it clean of info.

My job involved a bit of acting. I got out of the car and went to the first house in the circle and pretended to check the meters. Should someone ask what I was doing, I'd tell them I was looking for gas leaks by checking usage because our equipment was indicating a leak in the neighborhood. I had no idea if anyone would buy it. I was just banking on people's general ignorance of things.

On such a cold Sunday afternoon in mid-February, I was surprised to see so many kids outside playing. A brave one asked me what I was doing and I gave him my spiel.

"Is my house gonna blow up?"

I assured him it wasn't. No leaks so far, I told him.

When I got to Nussbaum's, I attached a special microphone designed to pick up sounds through walls to his window frame. I attached the wires to the transmitter box that would broadcast what the microphone picked up to the receiver in the car and made sure the transmitter box was camouflaged with snow. I then moved on to the next house and continued on around the circle until I had made my way back to the car.

Tina had gotten what she wanted from Nussbaum's cell and had turned on the receiver, which also had a recorder and a speaker. I got settled in the car and took a minute to figure out what I was hearing coming from the receiver's speaker. Nussbaum was apparently watching TV. Sounded like boxing.

"Find anything interesting on the cell?" I asked.

"A lot of text messages to Nicole. Looks like they're more than business associates and it's possible he's hoodwinking her, but I'd say it looks like he's genuinely in love with her. There are also calls to a number made around the time of Barlow's murder and

Celeste's shooting. Calls from the same number occur the day before Gary's murder and the attempt on Celeste's life."

"Did you try the number?"

"No. I want you to call. I think a man's voice will be better."

"Okay. What's the number?"

She showed me and I tapped the numbers into the phone. On the third ring the call went through and a voice said, "Passcode." I disconnected.

"The guy on the other end wanted a passcode."

"A passcode? Really?"

I nodded.

Tina stroked her chin. "This is interesting. Who would Nussbaum call and who would call him that there would have to be a passcode involved? He could very well be involved with the Yakuza. The fellow you called saw your number, didn't recognize it, and therefore asked for the passcode to make sure you were one of them."

"Makes sense, I guess."

Nussbaum's phone was ringing. He turned down the TV.

We heard, "Nuss—," followed by silence for fifteen or so seconds. Then, "Look, I told you. As soon as she's out of the hospital." A pause, followed by, "You'll get your money. Don't worry. I keep the books. Remember?" Another pause. "They won't bother you." Then there was a long span of silence before we heard Nussbaum's voice. "Holy shit. Are you kidding me? ... Of course not. All right, all right. I'm on it." The call must've ended for the TV got louder.

"Harry, call Melissa. We need a security detail pronto. One prepared for a night attack."

The tone of Tina's voice said it all. She was concerned. Very concerned.

29

END GAME

Sunday Night, 16-17 February

TINA AND I DECIDED TO TAKE A FORTY-SEVEN MINUTE BREAK, AFTER I called Melissa Olson for a security detail to be dispatched to home, sweet home, to visit a lavatory and buy something to eat at that sandwich shop which advertises free smells.

I know it's meant to be humorous, but how could they charge for the smell of their food? All smells are free. Well, on second thought, I guess there are some smells one might have to pay for. We gladly pay for aromatherapy smells. Anyway, the sandwich shop smells were indeed good and free and made me feel good about my purchase. Let's hear it for free smells.

We returned to the development and parked in a different spot, but still within sight of Nussbaum's house. Tina flipped the switch on the receiver and the speaker blurted out the sound of gunfire and explosions. Nussbaum probably hadn't gone anywhere in our absence. We unwrapped our sandwiches and began eating. The sandwiches were better than the smells. Mostly because they satisfied our hunger, but they were also very good sandwiches.

Using the data extraction device, Tina confirmed the phone

number which called our quarry earlier was the same number I had called and was asked to give a passcode.

"He's working for someone," Tina said in between bites of her Gargantuan, "and that someone I'm guessing is the Yakuza, who are hitting him up for a piece of the action in the bordello business."

"Makes sense," I replied.

"I'm also wagering he's going to attempt something nasty tonight in reprisal for my visit to who I'm guessing is his boss."

"I'm not betting against you. What I'm wondering is how he got involved with the Yakuza in the first place."

"That is a good question and one I don't have an answer for. Hopefully, we'll find out. Although, it doesn't matter. I just want this over."

The afternoon passed into night.

At half-past six, Melissa called and said she had a team in place and gave us a contact number.

Tina and I took turns with the night vision binoculars and listened to what was going on inside his house, which was nothing but noise from the television.

Just before eleven-thirty, things became very quiet in the Nussbaum household and at midnight the garage door went up and a black Buick Regal backed out of the garage and slowly down the driveway and out onto the street. I watched the door go down and tried to catch a glimpse inside the garage, but didn't see anything of note.

The sky was overcast and the night dark, save for the light from the few street lamps.

Nussbaum drove out of the cul-de-sac and out onto the street. I started the car and slowly followed without turning on my lights. When he was a block ahead of us, I turned on the lights and kept pace with him.

Tina called the number Melissa had given us. When Heloise answered, Tina told her to keep an eye out for a black Buick

Regal, but that our suspect might also ditch the car and arrive in a different vehicle or on foot. Heloise confirmed she understood.

He drove through the development and then turned south on Dunkirk Lane. When he reached County Road 6, he turned east. I kept back a half-dozen car lengths and hoped he didn't notice us. That of course is wishing a lot when one is out in the suburbs after midnight.

At the I-494 interchange he went south and then east on I-394. I think that's when he realized he had a tail. He suddenly stepped on the gas and we were doing ninety down the freeway. At the Ridgedale Mall exit he waited until the last moment and then took the ramp. I followed him around the ramp loop to Plymouth Road and watched him run a red light and speed off to the north on Plymouth.

"Leave it, Harry. Let's go home and see if he shows up there."

I got back on the freeway, took it into Minneapolis, and followed the city streets to the place we call home, where I pulled into the drive.

Helen and Heloise came up to the window and I rolled it down.

"We have two people stationed on the second floor, one to cover each street and the corner. We have four in cars covering the intersection, your drive, Franklin, and Irving. Another person is stationed in the clump of trees at your corner. Heloise is on the east porch, I'm on the front porch, and there is a person watching your back door."

Tina leaned over. "Thank you, Ladies."

"Don't mention it, Miss Wright."

They went back to their posts and I rolled up the window.

"Which direction do you think he'll come from, Harry?"

"If he comes at all."

"True, he might abort."

"Right." I thought a moment. "If he comes, the simplest route is Hennepin from the freeway. So probably from the east."

"He'd be spotted before he got to Irving."

"True, but he wouldn't necessarily know that."

"Correct."

I thought a moment, considering possible routes. "He might also come from the north or south on Irving."

"Possibly. And again he'd be spotted."

"He would and again he wouldn't know that."

"Why not the west, Harry?"

"The lake is there."

"Escape through the park would be easy, though."

"There is that. Hadn't thought of it. Too doggone old to be galavanting all over the countryside."

"I don't think Helen and Heloise considered a western approach likely, either. Park down at the corner of James. I'm guessing he'll come that way. From the west."

"Why?"

"Because I would."

I backed out of the drive, while Tina called Heloise and apprised her of the direction she thought Nussbaum would make his approach. When she disconnected from the call, she said, "Park on James south of Franklin at the corner."

I drove down to James, made a U-turn, and backed down the street. I was facing the wrong way, since James is a one-way going south, but at that time of the night, I'm not sure it mattered. Once parked, I cut the engine because we didn't want the exhaust plume to give us away or the engine noise. And there we waited while the cold began to seep into the car.

The car clock told me the time was eight after one in the morning. In five hours the rush hour traffic would begin. In outlying areas probably an hour earlier. If he was going to make his move he'd need to do so soon. Busy streets would impede his escape.

The temp inside a car gets cold fast when the wind is blowing and you're looking at wind chills between 0 and 10 degrees Fahrenheit. Sitting there in the Flex, waiting for Nussbaum, was no exception.

Tina and I had no need for night vision goggles due to ample light from the street lamps. She had her little Smith and Wesson .32 H&R Magnum revolver at the ready and I, my trusty old Smith Bodyguard revolver. I was hoping I wouldn't have to use it.

At just after half-past one, Tina broke out the hand warmers. They did in fact help the hands. My feet, though, were another story. Just before two, Tina quietly said, "There he is. He's carrying something." She phoned Heloise.

I saw him illuminated by the streetlight. He was heading east from Lake of the Isles, just as Tina had said. I switched the dome light to off so it wouldn't come on when we opened the doors, which we did slowly and got out of the car. We pushed them closed, but not so they'd latch and make noise.

He'd crossed the street to our side of Franklin and Tina moved out, crouched low, in a sprint after him. I followed her. The snow helped soften the sound of our footfalls. Unfortunately much had melted on the sidewalk and he must've heard something, for at the driveway which goes under Solstice's apartment, he ducked behind the wall and opened fire with a silenced submachine gun. Tina was on the ground and I dove into a mass of bushes. I'm sure the neighbors will be royally pissed. At the moment, though, their concern over the shrubs was not on my mind.

I heard two shots from Tina's revolver. I saw a muzzle flash and heard the report of a large caliber handgun from a car across the street. Then another gunshot, possibly from the house. And then there was silence.

30

JESUS WON'T BE WEEPING

Tuesday Afternoon, 18 February

THE POLICE CAME AND AN AMBULANCE, WHICH TOOK NUSSBAUM TO the hospital, around twenty minutes before three yesterday morning. Cal showed up shortly after and Tina delivered everything we had to him.

He was fuming. "Holding out again." He was so hot I was wondering if he'd bring on an early spring.

"I had to make sure it was complete."

"Complete my eye, Wright. You wanted a little limelight and maybe some revenge for your windows."

"What's the matter, Cal? You're pissed because you and your people missed the most important piece of evidence? You shouldn't be. With everything I've given you, if you play it right and get Nussbaum to sing — you get to take down the Yakuza before they get a strong foothold here. I'm doing you a big favor. Because… Because we're a team."

"Team? Is that what you call it? I have a partner. I don't need a team."

I could tell that one not only took Tina by surprise, it hurt one hell of a lot too.

"From now on, Wright, stay out of murder investigations. Stick to skip tracing and wayward spouses. Got it?"

"Sure. I get it, Lieutenant Swenson."

"Good. Because if you don't, you are going to lose your license. I will see to it. Do I make myself clear?"

When Tina didn't say anything, he turned around and stormed off.

That conversation took place around three or a little after yesterday morning. At ten, I called Feingold. He'd just gotten into the office. I told him the case was wrapped up, but there were complications.

"Prostitution? My client? The Reverend Celeste Barlow? Good God in heaven."

There was a pause and then he said, "Ought to get her off with probation if she'll turn State's evidence. Okay. Let me know if the retainer was enough."

"Yes, sir, I will."

And that was that. The case was closed. All that remained was the accounting and me typing up the official report.

At noon, the window guys showed up and went to work fixing the place up good as new.

This morning, the window guys were back at it by eight. Tina spent the day painting. I, typing. And Bea was at her desk reading *Ladies Home Journal*, listening to music, and waiting for the phone to ring.

Along about four in the afternoon, Feingold stopped by. We all gathered in the office to hear what he had to say.

"I heard from a lawyer friend of mine, who got it from one of the paralegals in the county attorney's office, that Nussbaum is singing a sweet song as part of some deal. Even as we speak, the police are rounding up the Yakuza members. Should make things very easy for me with Celeste."

In hearing him speak I was reminded of Celeste's comment: "Lawyers. They're like gossipy tenth grade girls."

"I'm sorry, Mr. Feingold," Tina said, "I had to turn the information regarding Celeste over to the police."

"Don't worry about it, Miss Wright. I understand that asshole Swenson was going to yank your license. You did what you had to do."

"Thank you for understanding."

"Don't mention it. Apparently this Nussbaum character and that crime syndicate go way back together. Hooked up with them when he was doing porn. He was their man on the scene to make sure they got their cut of the profits. When he hooked up with Celeste, he started forking over dough to them. The top guy made the connection between Celeste and Gary."

"What did Gary do that made them want to kill him?"

"Apparently he fell in love with some young gal who was going to be married off to one of their king pins. Tried to run away with the girl. They got caught and somehow he managed to get away."

Bea said, "Kind of like Romeo and Juliet."

Feingold laughed. "Kind of. Don't know what happened to the girl. We know what happened when they eventually found Barlow."

Tina's voice was soft when she spoke. "They probably disfigured her face and sent her back to her parents. Then she probably committed suicide."

Bea's hand went to her mouth and her eyes were like saucers. Feingold cleared his throat.

I shook my head. "David was right. Don't want to get on their bad side."

"It's the only side they have," Tina said. "There is nothing good about them."

"That's a sad story," Feingold said. "Hopefully the police get enough of them, hell, I hope they get all of them. We don't need any more gangs here."

"Hopefully," Tina concurred.

"Well, I have to run. As usual, Miss Wright, a pleasure doing business with you. And if that Swenson threatens you again, let me know. I have ways to make his life very uncomfortable. He should be thankful this city has you."

"Thank you, Mr. Feingold."

"Don't mention it. Have a good evening."

Feingold left. I saw him to the door and then returned to the office.

"Somebody loves you," I said.

Tina stood and left.

Bea and I sat there looking at each other.

"I guess I said the wrong thing."

"Yes, you did, Harry. What I really can't believe is how mean Cal was to her."

"I find it difficult to swallow myself. But facts are facts."

———

Night has come to Minneapolis. Our supper is over. Bea and I are in the living room sitting by the fire. Tina is in the music room playing Chopin's "Raindrop" Prelude. She hasn't said anything about Cal. She usually doesn't. However, Cal's response to her gift of Nussbaum and information was pretty harsh. I would have expected her to say something, but she has kept her response to herself.

Something happened between the time he stopped over on that Friday, ten nights ago, to tell us about the county attorney planning to charge Celeste and now. Something that ruffled feathers which looked as though they were all smooth.

This case has been a humdinger. Murder by seppuku. A minister turned high class hooker. A crime syndicate the connecting link between one murder and an attempted one. Then there was Cal and Tina going from so-so to not good and Tina coming to grips with no Jesus and having to deal on her own with whatever sins she has burdening her conscience.

I'm wondering what the future will bring. I know one thing, whatever the future does bring Jesus won't be weeping for us. We'll have to do that on our own, if need be.

EPILOGUE

On a Thursday, three weeks after the Barlow case came to a close, all was quiet in the Wright household. Cal hadn't moved back in, stopped by, or even called. Shoot, he could have at least sent an email or text message to her. Apparently there has been nothing. At least to my knowledge. While I didn't say anything, I felt something wasn't right. I know Bea felt it too and I suspect Tina did also, although if she was concerned she wasn't letting it show.

He's been angry with her before over her methods. This time, though, he truly went ballistic. I've known Cal for a few years now and that just wasn't him. He doesn't do that. His action fueled the thought in my mind someone was putting him up to it. I had a hunch who that someone might be, but I kept it to myself and just hoped he'd get over whatever was bugging him and keep to his earlier agreement with Tina. Because, in truth, I like Cal and Bea loves him. And both Bea and I think those two belong together.

The afternoon was pretty far gone. Tina was at her desk reading *Doctor Thorne* by Anthony Trollope. Bea was at hers tatting and listening to music. I was in the kitchen preparing Cock-a-leekie for supper.

The doorbell rang and, after a moment, I heard Bea answer the door. Her squeal of delight told me Cal had come calling. I wiped my hands and went to the outer office, but he'd already gone on to the inner office and closed the door.

"Something's wrong, Harry." Bea's voice was near a whisper.

"Turn on the speaker."

"Harry."

"Turn it on." We have hidden microphones in the Inner Sanctum and, if need be, Bea can listen in and record the conversation. There's also a listening post in the library, if we decide we need to be even more invisible.

Bea flipped the switch.

Tina's voice. Cold. "Who is she, Cal? Who are you fucking?"

"Tina."

"If you're going to end this, you can at least tell me the bitch's name. I want to know who's good enough for you, if I'm not."

Bea's hand flew to her mouth and her eyes were wide.

Cal's voice. Soft. "Nikki."

"Your partner? You threw me over for that goddamn whore of a partner you have?"

"Look, Tina. We get along. We don't have fights over stupid stuff, like coffee."

"Stupid? What I like and don't like is stupid? You bastard."

"Tina."

"Don't take one more step."

"Tina."

There was the sound of her desk drawer opening.

I whispered, "No, Tina. Don't do it."

We heard the racking of the slide.

"Get the hell out of my house and don't you ever come back."

"Put the gun down, Tina."

"Get out of my house. Now!" Her voice was strident.

We heard steps, the door flew open and he slammed it shut, paused a moment, and then Lieutenant Cal Swenson of

Minneapolis Homicide stormed out of the house without even so much as a glance in our direction.

Bea and I stared at each other, our mouths agape.

Over the speaker, we heard, "Why, Cal? I love you. Why do this?" And then Tina wept.

FROM ME TO YOU

I hope you enjoyed *But Jesus Never Wept.* If you did, please leave a review where you bought the book and on your favorite social media sites. Your review is like word of mouth advertising. And it is pure gold.

Become one of my VIP Readers! You'll get a free copy of *Vampire House and Other Early Cases of Justinia Wright, P.I.* and join the exciting and delicious world of Justinia Wright! You'll get curated and exclusive content, news, and other good stuff.

Sign up today for your free book at BookFunnel! Just click, tap, or scan the QR code!

CONTINUE THE ADVENTURE!

If you enjoyed *But Jesus Never Wept*, Tina and Harry's adventures continue in *The Conspiracy Game*.

Tina becomes a consultant to a political campaign to ferret out a spy from a rival campaign. And if that doesn't provide enough excitement, the murders certainly do.

Can Tina find the spy and the killer before she herself becomes the target? Find out in *The Conspiracy Game*. Politics in the land of Minnesota nice!

Click, tap, or scan the QR code to get your copy!

ALSO BY CW HAWES

I'm a multi-genre author, because more genres means more fun!

I currently have books in the mystery, horror/weird/paranormal, post-apocalyptic, and alternative history/dieselpunk genres.

Please take a look at the My Books page on my website to see all the worlds I inhabit and write about.

Just click, scan, or tap the QR code!

ABOUT CW HAWES

CW Hawes is a playwright, award winning poet, and fictioneer. He is also the author of the bestselling *Death Wears a Crimson Hat*.

His interests are wide ranging and this is reflected in both the genres and the contents of his books.

You can visit him at his website. Just click, tap, or scan the QR code.

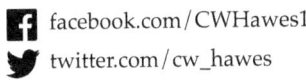

facebook.com/CWHawes1
twitter.com/cw_hawes